Was it wro... woman?

It didn't feel w... normal and right.

It wasn't as if Ann was still alive.

And he was. If he'd had any doubts about that in the past two years, today had dispelled them all. Yes, he was definitely alive – alive, well and in the market for a scorching affair.

Just sex, he promised himself. No commitment. Nothing long-term or permanent, just a little diversion to help ease life along a little. After all, the kids needed him and there was very little left over to give anybody else.

But an affair with Virginia – oh, yes. He could handle that.

HEARTBEAT

LOVE WHEN *LIFE* IS ON THE *LINE*

In the intense atmosphere of the Emergency department, dedicated medical professionals race against time to save patients' lives.

But can these men and women also find fulfilment in their own lives – and in each other's arms?

Lives lived heartbeat to heartbeat...

This special collection of sixteen books from some of Medical Romance's most exciting, emotional and intense authors offers you a glimpse into the life, love, passion and caring of the Emergency department.

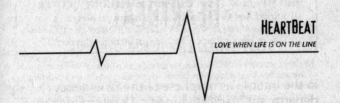

HEARTBEAT

LOVE WHEN LIFE IS ON THE LINE

THE PERFECT WIFE AND MOTHER?
Caroline Anderson

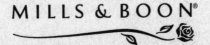

MILLS & BOON®

*First published in Great Britain 1997. This edition 2004.
Harlequin Mills & Boon Limited,
Eton House, 18-24 Paradise Road, Richmond, Surrey, TW9 1SR*

© Caroline Anderson 1997

ISBN 0 263 84483 8

142-0304

*Printed and bound in Spain
by Litografía Rosés S.A., Barcelona*

CHAPTER ONE

IT HAD been a good wedding.

Ryan was surprised. He'd been dreading it, in a way. Since Ann had died, weddings weren't his favourite thing. He was OK till they got to the 'till death do us part' bit, then he was inclined to go to pieces inside.

Strangely, this time he hadn't. Time healing and all that? Maybe. Maybe it was just because Jill and Zach so obviously belonged together. Maybe it was because this time the children had been with him and had been fidgety and he'd had to entertain them. Maybe it was all sorts of things that he couldn't account for.

Whatever the reason, it had been a lovely wedding. He shrugged into his white coat, peered at his reflection in the little mirror behind the door and finger-combed his hair.

It was too short, really, but it had been so hot and he'd had it cut for the wedding. It sprang back now, tawny and rebellious—streaked paler by the sun—and he gave up. When it was longer he'd be able to make it co-operate. For now, it just stuck up with that wiry kink in it and that was the way it was. Still, it suited him in a way, made him look younger than his thirty-five years. He searched his face thoughtfully. Was he imagining it or were the lines of grief fading?

About time. It had been two years now, just over. Two long, lonely, heartbreaking years. The children had been more accepting of Ann's death, but he'd challenged God at every turn. It hadn't helped. He'd still woken up every morning alone.

Perhaps it was time to change that. A little light flirta-tion, perhaps? Maybe an affair? Nothing wild, just a dis-creet liaison with a woman who understood the rules.

A bit of ego-massage.

Yeah.

He grinned at himself—pleased with the idea—and his eyes sparkled back, green light dancing in their depths.

A woman. His gut tightened at the thought, and he chuckled softly. Would he even remember what to do?

Ginny found the accident and emergency department and looked around. Already, at eight-thirty in the morning, it was bustling with life.

Good. She couldn't bear standing around all day with nothing to do. That was why she'd chosen A and E. Now to find her boss.

It wasn't difficult. She sort of fell over him, really. One minute she was walking along the corridor minding her own business and wondering where she should go to find him, the next a door opened and a tall, fair-haired man walked smack into her path.

Literally.

His hands came up and grabbed her shoulders, her breasts bounced off his iron-hard chest, and sensation ex-ploded inside her.

Heat—Lord, yes, such heat! Not body heat but power, coiled energy, sheer sex appeal. And strength, from the hands gripping her shoulders to steady her to the muscles of his chest bunching beneath her flattened palms. Gentle-ness, too, his hands relaxing instantly but staying there—cupping her shoulders with their long, blunt fingers.

Stunned, confused for a second, and yet unwillingly fas-cinated, Ginny stepped back and looked up—and found herself transfixed by the most astonishingly green eyes she had ever seen.

Funny, they hadn't seemed so green at her interview. And now, she realised, they were more than green. They were interested.

'Dr O'Connor?' she murmured. 'I'm Virginia Jeffries, your new SHO—your new Resident.'

Ryan felt as if he'd been hit over the head by a rock. One minute he was dreaming of a woman—any woman—to lighten his life, and the next minute—bang!—there was a woman in his arms.

And what a woman! Soft, cloud-grey eyes framed by long black lashes untainted by mascara, dark glossy hair swinging sleekly to her chin, a soft, full mouth curved in a smile of greeting—he might as well die now and go to heaven.

Had she really been so lovely at her interview? He didn't remember. How strange that he could have been unaware of her as a woman. Impossible. Lord, he must have been unconscious at the time!

He remembered himself and let her go, stepping back out of harm's way and sucking in his first breath for almost half a minute. 'Um—hi, there,' he managed inanely, and could have kicked himself. Damn, had it really been so long since he'd chatted up a woman that he couldn't remember how to talk to one?

Yes—but more to the point she was a junior colleague, and he would do well to remember that. No cosying up to this one, no matter how good she might feel squashed up against his chest.

His body was busy disagreeing. He buttoned his coat to allow it a little privacy until he had time to argue about it. Meanwhile he had work to do and an impression to create—if he could just unscramble his tonsils and get the words out!

'Ah—call me Ryan, please? And can I call you Virginia?' Wow, what a smile! He could feel his socks beginning to smoulder.

'Do—or Ginny. Whichever.'

He nodded. He had to. His brain had disconnected from his tongue and gone walkabout. He cleared his throat. 'Ah—right, well if you'll come with me we'll see what we can do. You'll need a coat—'

'I got one at Reception.'

'—and a stethoscope?'

'Here.'

She waggled it at him and he nodded. Lord, her grin was delicious. 'Fine,' he croaked. 'Right. Let's go and find some patients.'

He was lovely. Dreadfully uncomfortable, fascinated by her, embarrassed by his reaction—what a sweetheart! And she had to admit to a certain fascination herself. What healthy woman wouldn't? He wasn't conventionally handsome, but his craggy good looks and wonderful green eyes had a definite masculine appeal.

And that voice—soft, deep, a little gruff, with a slow drawl that put his origins from across the pond—Canada, perhaps? His speech was quite precise—or would have been if he'd been able to get his tongue off the roof of his mouth! Poor man. Hormones could be quite ruthless.

She didn't remember his voice from the interview. Perhaps he hadn't said a great deal. She seemed to remember that it had been Jack Lawrence who had done most of the talking. She was sure she would have remembered if Ryan had said much, with that smoky, gravelly voice just made for loving—

A shiver ran down her spine and she sighed. It was a shame he was a colleague. She didn't like muddying the waters with personal matters.

Still, for him perhaps she could make an exception...?

She followed his broad, straight back down the corridor and round into the hub of the treatment area. There were trolleys with patients on, cubicles with people sitting and lying in varying states of undress and distress, and nurses bustling busily from one to the other, quietly efficient.

And once there, of course, they were instantly in demand. A nurse showed her the staffroom where she could stow her bag, and she slipped on her coat, hung her stethoscope round her neck and went back out into the fray.

'Here.' Ryan handed her a badge that said, DR VIRGINIA JEFFRIES—SHO, and she pinned it to her lapel, grinned at him and looked around.

'Where do we start?'

'Over here,' he said. He sounded better now, more in command of himself, his words precise and yet spoken with that lovely soft transatlantic drawl that made her skin shiver.

He picked up a file from a stack on a table. 'I think for the morning you'd better stick close to me and see how things work,' he said, and then turned away—but not before she saw recognition of the double meaning of his words strike home.

She nearly chuckled. The skin on the back of his neck warmed to a delicate shade of brick, and her grin wouldn't be suppressed. If she'd got much closer to him she would have known exactly how things worked, she thought mischievously. She schooled her face into a businesslike mask and kept her chuckle private.

There would be plenty of time for jokes once she knew him better!

* * *

The morning removed the urge to laugh. Instead, she wanted to scream with frustration because, despite the early bustle the work died to a trickle and she was forced to stand around like a fourth-year student and watch the maestro at work.

It would have been a good idea if she'd been able to concentrate on taking in all the technical detail, like where the X-ray request forms were kept and who did the strapping on the sprains and which nurse did the casts and where the vomit bowls were in an emergency!

Instead, she watched his hands, long and strong, the fingers careful but thorough as he explored injuries. She studied his bent head, the hair short-cropped and springy—the ends tipped blond by the sun.

And she listened to his voice, and the warm, melodious flow of it lulled her into a sensuous daze.

But still she did no work, put her hands on no one, wasted a morning.

Ginny didn't like wasting time—even time spent admiring Ryan O'Connor. She was glad, then, when things started to hot up a little and she actually got to examine a cut for fragments of glass and, wonder of wonders, examine, diagnose and admit an elderly lady with a Colles' fracture of her wrist.

She was just about to lance an infected abscess on a young woman's finger when the nurse popped her head round the cubicle curtain and told her that there were two coming in on a blue light, and could she stand by in Resuscitation with Ryan as Jack Lawrence, the other consultant, was busy with a cardiac arrest and couldn't be spared, and Patrick Haddon, the SR, was similarly occupied with a child with severe burns?

'I think they're critical,' she told Ginny. 'Ryan's on the phone to the paramedic in the ambulance, giving him instructions about one of them—could you come and talk to the other one?'

There was hardly time, though, because no sooner had she excused herself from the patient she was treating than they heard the sound of sirens entering the hospital grounds.

All hell broke loose then. The doors were held open, the trolleys brought in at a run and Ryan was working on the first casualty before they entered the resuscitation room. Ginny just had time to register masses of frothy blood around the girl's face before her own patient was there under her nose.

The second trolley was pulled up parallel with the first, and the paramedic gave her a quick breakdown of the findings.

'Motorbike accident,' he said unnecessarily, as the lad was still wearing his leathers although his helmet had been removed. 'Unconscious at the scene, hasn't regained consciousness. Left leg is splinted—it's very deformed in the lower third of the femur, but it looks like a closed fracture. Don't know about spinal injuries but it's possible. We put a backboard on to make sure, but we couldn't leave the helmet on because we needed to get an airway in.'

She nodded. 'OK. Thank you.'

While he was talking she checked the patient's airway and ensured that it was working, and then frowned. His breathing was laboured and she was concerned about his chest.

'Can we get these clothes off him, please?'

'Put him on a sliding plate trolley first so we can X-ray him *in situ*,' Ryan said from across the room.

So they shifted him with extreme care to support his head and neck in a neutral position, and then the splint was taken off his leg and his clothes were cut away to reveal his injuries.

'If he lives he'll complain like mad about this,' the nurse working alongside Ginny said with a grin as she sliced up the side of the expensive leather gear the man was wearing.

'Let's just hope he lives to complain,' Ginny muttered under her breath, and then ran her eyes over each part of him as it was revealed.

As the paramedic had said, his femur was distorted just above the knee and his right wrist looked very strange, but it was his chest that Ginny was concerned about. The left side was not inflating properly and when she pressed down gently she could feel the crepitations of the bone-ends scraping together.

'Lower ribs, have gone on the left—I think he's got a punctured lung,' she told Ryan.

'Watch him for shock—the spleen might have gone too,' Ryan mumbled, and then swore as his patient began to shudder and convulse. 'Damn—I need to get this airway sorted,' he growled.

Ginny tuned him out and concentrated on her patient. His pupils were equal and reactive to light, which she was grateful for, but he didn't respond at all to voice and only slightly to pain.

She recorded the information on a neurological observation chart because of the suspected head injury, but she was more concerned for the moment with the immediate problem of his chest and abdomen.

She put in two chest drains—one for air and one for blood—using local anaesthetic in case he could feel it but not react, and asked the nurse for a report on his status as she watched the steady ooze of blood from the lower chest drain. She was glad she'd done it before. Now was not the time to learn!

'Pulse one-twenty, thready, blood pressure seventy over thirty and falling.'

'Damn. Let's get some IV lines in and fill him up a bit. Is the X-ray coming?'

The door opened then and the radiographer came in. They worked round her, Ginny refusing to step back and continuing to put in the IV line into his left arm while the pictures were taken.

'You shouldn't do that—you're a young woman,' the radiographer scolded gently.

'Don't worry about me, I'm fine,' Ginny said shortly, withdrawing some of the precious blood for cross-matching. 'Can we have the chest results quickly, please?'

'Sure.'

They were left in peace then, squeezing the plasma expander in fairly rapidly to bulk up his blood volume while they waited for cross-matching. His blood pressure picked up a little, and they inserted another line into his damaged right arm.

'I don't want to use his legs because of the femur injury and possible internals,' she said to Ryan, 'and the neck I want to avoid until we're sure he hasn't got a head injury, so is it OK to use this broken arm?'

'You've got no choice,' he told her absently. 'That's more like it. OK, aspirate, please; get the blood out of her trachea. Can you cope, Virginia?'

'Yes, I think so.'

'Get four units of blood into him stat—use O neg while you wait for cross-match. There should be some coming up.'

There was, and she was glad to see it. Her patient's pulse was very weak and thready, although they had boosted his blood volume, and she wondered how much he was losing into the thigh and how much through what she was beginning to be sure was a ruptured spleen.

'Should we do a peritoneal lavage to see if he's haemorrhaging?' she asked Ryan.

He shook his head. 'No. Treat as if he is—there should be a general surgeon on his way down to check. If he's not here in five minutes—or if the lad deteriorates—I'll stick a needle in and see what we come up with. Better catheterise him anyway—he's going to have to go to the operating theatre. Do we have any ID?'

The nurse lifted her head from the catheter she was already inserting. 'Yes. The police are on it, apparently. They're contacting relatives now.'

A man came in then, tall and rangy, his white hair in sharp contrast to the bushy black brows beneath. 'Query abdomen for me?' he said in a soft Scottish burr.

'Oh, hi, Ross. Yeah, Virginia's got it. She'll fill you in.'

She met his eyes and smiled briefly. 'Hi. I think his spleen might have gone. His ribs have penetrated his left lung low down, but he's also got a possible head injury and his left femur and right wrist have gone.'

Ross nodded. 'OK. Can I have a trocar, please?'

He scrubbed quickly while they prepared the abdomen for his incision, then Ginny watched as he carefully pushed the sharp instrument into the abdomen and pressed gently.

Blood welled rapidly out of the little hole, far too much and too fast to be because of the incision.

'Damn. Right, we'd better have him now. Have we got head and spinal X-rays?'

'Just done.' They were snapped up on the light box by the radiographer, and Ross scanned them quickly. 'That looks OK. Right, we can assume his head injury is of secondary importance to his internal haemorrhaging. The spleen looks enlarged and the abdo contents are displaced—aye, I'm sure it's gone. I'll get the orthopaedic boys to sort his leg and arm out after I've finished with the spleen and chest. How stable is he?'

'Not bad,' Ginny replied. 'I think he's improving. He's certainly not getting any worse, but his blood pressure's still a bit low.'

Ross nodded. 'OK. Can you send him up as soon as he's stable enough, please? I'll go and scrub. How about this one?'

Ryan grunted. 'Smashed mandible, lacerated tongue— I'm just suturing it now to stop the bleeding. Apart from that and the coma and the leg fractures, she's fine.'

Ross snorted and left the room.

Ginny's patient's parents arrived at that point, so he was covered with a blanket; Ginny warned them about the breathing tube and the chest drains and IV lines, and then they came in for a few moments.

They were shocked and upset but, as Ryan said later, at least they knew he was still alive and recognisable, which was more than could be said for the girl who had been on the back of his bike. Her facial injuries were extensive and would require the intervention of a plastic surgeon—if she survived the head injury. Ryan thought her helmet must have been too big for her, as it had come off at the scene. Either that or it had been ripped off, thus damaging her jaw.

The boy's parents were distressed by her condition, as well as their son's. It seemed they were going out together and had been for some time.

'Do you know where the police might find her parents?' Ryan asked them.

'Possibly.'

'Would you talk to them? The nurse has some forms for you to sign first, then if you could talk to the police?'

'Of course.' With shaking hands they signed the consent form for surgical treatment of their son's various injuries and, as Ginny was happy with his blood pressure and pulse, he went off to the operating theatre.

Ryan's patient, on the other hand, was still causing concern. The fragments of her fractured lower jaw had penetrated her mouth and tongue and were causing serious problems. Ryan had been unable to get an airway in and had had to do a tracheostomy to allow her to breathe because of the blood in her throat and her swollen tongue, but he had been able to suture the worst cut on the tongue to halt the outpouring of blood into the back of her throat that was threatening to drown her.

Her parents hadn't yet arrived, but she was at least stable now. Ginny went over to Ryan and asked if she could help.

He grinned tiredly. 'No, not really. You could finish off that patient you abandoned. I'll be through here in a minute and she'll be transferred to the intensive therapy unit. I'll come with you if you hang on.'

Ginny had quite forgotten the woman whose infected finger she had been about to lance. 'It seems hours ago,' she murmured.

'Only half an hour.'

He was still working. Ginny watched him as he checked the girl's pupils again. 'How's her head injury?'

'Not good. Her pupils are both equal and reacting, but she's still very deep. She's got multiple fractures in both legs and one arm, but all in all she's got away with it lightly if the head injury isn't anything too sinister. I think she was wrapped round a tree branch, from what I can gather. It may be just whiplash or it may be worse. She's got a nasty cut on her leg as well. She'll need a tetanus jab.'

He did that as they talked, and Ginny was able to see

the long, jagged cut up her thigh. 'Are you going to stitch it?' she asked.

He looked horrified. 'No. It's dirty—we'll pack it and leave it for a few days with antibiotics, then it can be sutured on the ward. If you close it now you trap all that road dirt in it and she'd get a nasty infected wound for sure.'

Ginny suddenly felt the yawning void of her ignorance opening up under her feet. 'Sorry,' she mumbled.

Ryan lifted his head and met her eyes over the patient, and grinned. 'Don't apologise. That's why you're working with me—to learn these things. You did really well with that lad, by the way. Well done.'

His eyes glowed with appreciation, and Ginny felt as if the sun had come out from behind the clouds.

All the blood and gore receded and, as she returned his smile, her confidence came back and she straightened up.

'Thanks,' she murmured, and her voice sounded husky and emotional. 'Um—what now?'

'Your lady?' he prodded gently.

She laughed and pulled herself together. 'Oh. Right.'

She was heading out of the door when his pointed cough stopped her in her tracks.

'Try removing some of the blood before you go out there,' he said mildly.

She looked down at her coat, fresh this morning, and her eyes widened in surprise. 'Mmm—I see what you mean.'

Ryan's patient was collected and taken to Theatre while she cleaned herself up, and he joined her at the sink. Their eyes met in the mirror.

'Shall we finish off that poor woman now?' she said.

His grin was worth waiting for.

'She's probably got better on her own by now, but I suppose we ought to check.'

Chuckling, they left the devastation behind, and the team of nursing staff waded in for the clean-up, ready for the next onslaught—whenever that might be. While the nurses checked the instruments and relaid the trolleys and prepared the room, Ryan and Ginny discovered that another doctor had taken over and finished treating Ginny's patient, so they went into the staffroom. While a fresh pot of coffee brewed Ryan talked her through the treatment both their biker patients would go on to receive. Then, just as the coffee-machine chugged and spluttered to a halt, they heard a siren again.

Ryan looked at her with those extraordinary green eyes and arched a brow expressively. 'We're on again,' he murmured. 'You stay here and have a coffee, if you like; I'll handle it.'

'Are you being kind or was that a dismissal?'

He grinned. 'Dismissal? You have to be kidding. I tell you what—you go and see to it, I'll have the coffee.'

She got instantly to her feet. 'I tell you what—we'll both go and deal with it and we'll both have a coffee!'

Well, as first days went, it had been a good one, Ginny mused. She kicked off her shoes, dropped tiredly onto her extremely comfortable bed and closed her eyes. Thank God she wasn't on duty that night. She wouldn't have been at her best, although she would have done it as she'd done it countless times over the past couple of years.

She replayed the day—or, at least, she meant to, but she didn't get a great deal further than Ryan.

Ryan's voice, Ryan's laugh, Ryan's hands on her shoulders. Ryan's chest squashed up against hers—well, the other way round to be exact, as Ryan's chest wouldn't squash with anything as trivial as her impact on it. Hers, on the other hand, had squashed most convincingly. She peered down at her bust, full and ripe and overtly feminine, and wondered how Ryan's hands would feel gently cupping that softness.

A dull ache started up behind her eyes. She was tired. She must be, to start imagining things like that about her new boss. After all, after that first initial contact, he'd been very circumspect and had kept his distance both physically and verbally.

No little jokes, no innuendo—nothing to give her any indication that the attraction she thought she'd seen in his eyes had been anything other than her imagination or a fleeting interest dispelled by time and further exposure.

Which was just as well—wasn't it? And, anyway, he was probably married.

'Did you have a good day today?'

Evie nodded, her eyes wide and sparkling with mischief. 'Granny took us to the beach again. We had ice cream and went on the little train and Gus was sick from eating too much popcorn.'

Ann's mother smiled apologetically. 'I don't think it's anything to worry about. Children are often sick if they overindulge. I shouldn't have let him have so much, should I, Angus?'

Gus shook his head cheerfully. 'My sick was all full of popcorn and bright green from my lolly—'

'OK, Gus, we don't need the details,' Ryan said wearily. How many times had he told their grandmother not to spoil them so much? They always had too much sun, too much food, too much everything. He hustled them to the car, strapped them in and took them home, tired but happy, and decided he was being too strict. So what if she spoiled

them a little? They were kids. God knows, they had little
enough fun in their lives.

It was funny how bathtime and bedtime always seemed
endless, and yet when it was done and the children were
tucked up in bed sound asleep the evening seemed to
stretch on into the hereafter.

He showered and changed into old jeans and a scruffy
T-shirt, meaning to tackle the garden a little before he went
to bed, but it was a gorgeous evening and he found himself
sitting down after his solitary meal with a beer in one hand
and the local paper in the other, enjoying the last of the
evening sun—and thinking about Virginia.

Lord, she was pretty. Her soft, lush curves had squashed
up against him most invitingly, and he really hadn't
wanted to let her go. He'd forgotten what a real woman
felt like—how solid and robust and positively right.

His heart started to thud more heavily, just with the
memory, and his jeans tightened to an embarrassing de-
gree. He closed his eyes and tipped his head back against
the sun lounger and sighed. Was it wrong to want another
woman? It didn't feel wrong. It felt frighteningly normal
and right.

It wasn't as if Ann was still alive.

And he was. If he'd had any doubts about that in the
past two years, today had dispelled them all. Yes, he was
definitely alive—alive, well and in the market for a scorching affair.

Just sex, he promised himself. No commitment. Nothing
long-term or permanent, just a little diversion to help ease
life along a little. After all, the kids needed him and there
was very little left over to give anybody else.

But an affair with Virginia—oh, yes. He could handle
that.

She's a colleague, his alter ego was nagging gently. He

switched it off. She understood the rules. She was a woman of the world—that was obvious from the assessing look she had given him that had thrown him for a loop.

They could work together and play together.

It would be fine. He'd make it fine.

His heart thudded a little faster, the beat heavy and strong under his ribs.

Anticipation.

He'd forgotten the taste of it, it had been so long.

He'd flirt with her a little, draw her out, see if she was interested. Maybe dinner, a play or the movies—something like that.

He wondered how Ann's mother would feel about babysitting for him while he entertained a new woman.

Perhaps he'd ask the girl next door…!

CHAPTER TWO

So MAYBE she'd been mistaken. Maybe Ryan was interested. Either that or she was reading him all wrong, which could be fairly embarrassing!

She wasn't. Every chance he had he made eye contact with her, and his eyes were ultra-expressive. She wasn't sure if he meant them to be or if they just gave him away, but he was certainly interested in her.

She still didn't know anything about him, however, but she was willing to bet from what she'd seen of him at work that he wasn't the sort of man to cheat on his wife. The easy thing, of course, was just to come out and ask him, but she didn't like to.

It was Patrick Haddon, one of the senior registrars, who told her in the end. They'd been working together on a patient and as the trolley was wheeled away to the ward he stripped off his gloves, dropped them in the bin and grinned at her.

'Well done. I can see why Ryan speaks so highly of you—apart from the obvious attraction he feels, of course.'

His eyes were twinkling, and Ginny felt a soft tide of colour brush her throat. She ignored the compliment on her work in favour of the rider he had added. 'Meaning?' she fished.

Patrick laughed softly. 'Don't tell me you haven't noticed the way he looks at you.'

She shrugged, pretending indifference. 'Is it so obvious?'

'It is to me. It makes a change to see him notice the sex

of his colleagues. Not that anybody's criticising, Ginny. We're all vulnerable to the right pretty face. Anyway, it's good to see him taking an interest in a woman. Two years is a long time.'

'Two years?' she asked, trying not to let her curiosity be too obvious.

'Since his wife died. I don't think there's been anyone since.'

She felt the shock of his words in a wave of regret for Ryan. How had she died? Slowly, or instantly? Did he know it was going to happen? Did he have time to say goodbye? How much had he been hurt?

So many questions without answers. There was only one Patrick could answer that she was prepared to ask, and even that was a loaded question. 'Did they have children?' she asked slowly.

'Yes—two. A girl and a boy.'

Ginny felt a pang. She wasn't sure which was worse— to have them and die, or live and not have them.

To die. Yes, of course. Her life was full, after all. Her work was demanding, interesting and stimulating. Her private life was about to flourish, if Ryan's eyes were to be believed, and everything in her garden was rosy.

Well, almost. There was that little corner where nothing grew—where nothing would ever grow—but it was engulfed by the glorious mass of busyness that threatened to swamp her on occasions.

Yes, it was good to be alive.

Far better than to be dead.

Or widowed. Poor Ryan. She wondered what and when he would tell her about it. Probably not a lot, as he hadn't yet. She sensed that his private life and work were kept very far apart, and she wondered which slot she would be fitted into if she became his mistress.

A third slot, kept especially for that eventuality? Neither one thing nor the other? Category Three—sex slave.

She gave a short, humourless laugh. 'Don't count your chickens, Patrick,' she warned him. 'Or Ryan's. Not that it's anybody else's business, but I'm sure if he was that interested he would have done something about it by now.'

But he hadn't, and he didn't, and by the end of that week she was wondering if he ever would.

He was constantly underfoot, though. On the pretext of training her he was there at her side all the time, and by the end of Friday she was ready to hit him. She was off duty at five, much to her great relief, and she went into the staffroom to hang up her coat. As she came out so he came in, and their chests collided just as before.

This time, though, he didn't release her but stared down into her eyes and kept her there, hard against his body, while his eyes smouldered like green coals and her pulse rate rocketed.

She met his hungry gaze frankly, and after a few moments his eyes dropped to her mouth. She thought he was going to kiss her. Most men would have, but Ryan clearly had more control.

She wished to God he didn't, but it was probably just as well because there were people passing them in the corridor and they were attracting some very strange and interested looks.

'Did you want something?' she asked softly, and under her hands his chest jerked a fraction. A sharp intake of breath?

His eyes flicked up to hers again, and the heat in them made her own breath jerk in response. 'Um—yeah, actually,' he said hesitantly, 'I was wondering if you were doing anything tomorrow night?'

Someone barged past them and his body was nudged against hers. It felt good—too good to miss.

She smiled slowly. 'What did you have in mind?' She could have sworn his skin coloured, just slightly. Guilt? She suppressed a chuckle.

'Um—dinner? Perhaps the cinema? There's a new film on I've been wanting to see, but I'm easy.'

'Sounds fine,' she said with a smile. 'What time?'

He looked flummoxed for a moment. 'Time? Ah— seven? I'll pick you up—where do you live?'

'Here—at the hospital. I've got one of those poky little rooms, but as I'm only in it for ten minutes at a time it doesn't matter. I'll meet you at the main entrance.'

'Fine. Seven o'clock tomorrow, then.' As if he finally realised that he was standing pressed up against her he backed off a step then, with a slow grin, he released her and turned away. As he walked off down the corridor she heard him whistling softly under his breath, as if he was pleased with himself.

Smiling, she made her way back to her little room, flung the window open to let in some fresh air and examined the sparse contents of her wardrobe.

Nothing. She needed a shopping trip. Excellent!

Ryan thought he must have lost his marbles. First of all he'd grabbed her like a sex-starved adolescent, then he'd hung on and forgotten to let go of her because the feel of those soft breasts had been enough to curdle the remaining fragments of his mind. And, as if that wasn't bad enough, he'd gone and done what he'd spent all week trying to stop himself from doing, and invited her out tonight.

He yanked the tie off in exasperation. It was too hot to wear a tie. It was too hot to wear anything. It was certainly too hot for the sort of frenzied activity his body had in mind.

He yanked off the rest of his clothes, took a deep breath and got back into the cold shower. That would settle his little friend down, he thought viciously. He was *not* going to jump her bones on the first date. He was *not!* No, sir. Or the second.

Maybe not even the third.

Well, OK, the third. Damn. His body had cheered up again, despite the cold water.

He swore as he wrenched the curtain back again and grabbed a towel, just as Evie wandered into the bathroom. 'I thought you were in bed, sweetheart?' he said to her, rapidly covering the evidence of his outrageously optimistic libido.

'I was. I'm too hot. Daddy, you said a bad word.'

He closed his eyes. 'I know. I'm sorry, honey. I'm feeling hot too.' Well, at least it wasn't a lie. He crouched down and took her hands in his. 'Want me to read you a story?'

She nodded. 'Gus is asleep already.'

'I thought he would be. He was tired after our walk. What shall we read?'

'*Black Beauty,*' she said without hesitation.

He sighed. She was going to be into horses whether he encouraged her or not, he realised. Oh, well, there were worse things. He'd grown up around horses—heck, his brother was a Mountie. It was safer than drugs. 'OK, *Black Beauty,*' he agreed, and they settled down on her bed and he started to read.

Ten minutes later, as her eyes began to droop, the door-bell rang.

'That'll be the babysitter. You look at the pictures and I'll get her to read to you some more.'

'Why couldn't Granny come?' Evie asked as he headed for the door, still clad in just the towel.

'Ah—I just thought we'd give her the night off.'

'Are you going out with a lady?'

What the hell did he say to that? 'Um—in a way,' he flannelled. 'I work with her—we're going to talk about work.'

And he ran downstairs, waiting for a thunderbolt to strike him down for lying to his six-year-old daughter.

The neighbour's seventeen-year-old daughter eyed his naked chest with interest. 'Am I early, or are you just late?' she asked frankly.

He coloured a little. 'I'm just late. I was reading to Evie. Come in, Suzannah. Would you go up and finish reading the chapter to her while I throw on some things? Thanks.'

He led her upstairs, ushered her into Evie's room and then shot into his room and grabbed his clothes. There was no time to be selective now. Taupe chinos, cream cotton shirt without tie, blazer, tie in pocket just in case. Wallet. Comb hair—for what it was worth. Shoes—no, not work shoes. Neutral suede desert boots. It was too hot for anything else. Right.

He kissed Evie, checked Gus, told Suzannah he would be back about eleven, gave her his mobile number and ran.

He was late. Ginny checked her watch, glanced once more down the drive towards the main vehicular entrance and went and sat down on a low wall by the door.

Her skirt was fortunately multicoloured and wouldn't show the marks, but after shopping all day in the hideous heat the last thing she wanted was to stand.

She plucked at the soft, crinkle-pleated cotton of the skirt and wondered if it was as transparent as she suspected

with the light behind it. Not that there'd be any light behind it if he was much later.

Oh, well. It was delicate and feminine and made her feel
good, and she had a snug vest-top on under a wispy blouse
that matched the skirt, the tails tied at her waist. It exag-
gerated her bust a little too much, but so what? It was her
best asset. She might as well use it.

Her fingers plucked at the skirt again. She hoped it
looked as good as it felt, and that it would be formal
enough for whatever he had in mind.

Whatever it was, she hoped that it included food early
in the programme because she hadn't eaten since breakfast
and that had been a rather scratch affair.

A dark blue estate car came into view, doing horrible
things to the site speed limit of ten miles an hour, and
pulled up right beside her. Ryan jumped out and came over
to her, looking rueful and good enough to eat.

'Sorry I'm late—domestic hiccup. All set?'

She nodded and stood up, and judged her money wisely
spent. His reaction was a peach. His jaw sagged a little,
his eyes widened and fastened like limpets on her exag-
gerated bust, and with a conscious effort he dragged his
gaze up to her face and cleared his throat slightly.

'You look—very—um…' he managed. He closed his
eyes and gave a rueful laugh. 'Sorry. That white coat
covers up a lot. You look stunning. I'm stunned. Really.'

She chuckled softly. 'You're no slouch yourself,
O'Connor.'

He grinned, his equilibrium under control again, opened
the car door for her, tucked her skirt in and closed it before
striding round and sliding behind the wheel. 'Right—what
would you like to do? Movies or dinner first?'

She pulled an apologetic face. 'Dinner? I'm starving.'

'So am I. Formal or informal?'

'Informal.'

'Inside or out?'

She laughed. 'Out, for preference.'

'Done. There's a pub that serves excellent food and they've got a riverside garden with willow trees. It's really beautiful and cool too, which has to be a plus.'

'Just lead the way,' she said with a smile, and leant back against her seat. He liked the clothes. Good. And he was going to feed her. Life was wonderful.

The pub garden was busy, but as they went outside with their drinks a couple sitting under one of the trees got up to leave and vacated the secluded little spot.

Glad that her skirt wouldn't show the grass stains, Ginny sat down, wrapped her arms round her legs and propped her chin on her knees. The willow branches hung like a curtain around them, whispering in the slight evening breeze, and although they were surrounded by people it was as if they were alone.

They were close to the water's edge, and there were ducks lazily holding their position against the current and waiting hopefully for a crust or the odd chip. Ginny watched them for a moment then with a chuckle turned to Ryan, to find him watching her again with a strange intensity.

She expected him to flush or turn away, but he didn't. Instead, his eyes burned into hers. 'You're beautiful, Virginia,' he murmured, and she was the one who blushed. 'Beautiful and feminine and very, very tempting. I made myself a promise tonight.'

She waited and eventually he continued, his voice strained, 'I promised myself I wasn't going to jump your bones. Not on the first date, at least, or the second.'

'When's the third?' she asked brazenly, shocked at herself but unable to help the words.

His eyes darkened and his breath caught in his throat. 'Dammit, woman, you aren't supposed to say things like that!' he choked out on a laugh.

She laughed with him, caught up in the sensual cocoon of their living hideaway, and he moved closer, turning sideways so that he was sitting on one hip with his leg drawn up and leaning on his outstretched hand—leaving the other hand free to give her its undivided attention.

His knuckles grazed her cheek, just softly, then down over the hollow of her throat until the backs of his fingers rested against the swell of her breast, just visible over the scooped neck of the little top.

Then his hand turned over, skimming across her breast and up, so that his fingers lay against the pulse at the side of her neck and his thumb dragged sensuously over her waiting lips. He caught her chin to steady her, and then his mouth was descending slowly, closing with hers inch by tormenting inch.

That first touch of his mouth was like the brush of an angel's wing—light, delicate, almost her imagination.

And then he kissed her, and the world outside their shimmering curtain disappeared in a haze of sensation. He was still gentle, but there was no part of her that felt untouched by him in the course of that one sweet kiss. Her lips parted for his tongue, and it seemed to caress her soul. No one had ever kissed her like that—ever.

She didn't want it to end, but of course it did. Good things always did—and this one with a muttered oath.

'Number thirty-seven?' a girl was calling.

'Damn,' he said again. 'That's our supper. Virginia, would you? I can't go out there like this.'

He looked embarrassed, but he didn't need to. She was every bit as aroused. It was just more subtle. She stood up,

ducked under the willow curtain and retrieved their food
from the waitress.

When she went back under the tree he was sitting with
his leg hitched up, one arm resting on his knee and the
other wrapped round his shin. He looked awkward, as if
the kiss had been an accident, and she couldn't bear to see
him flagellate himself for the most beautiful experience of
her life.

She sat down, passed him his supper and met his rueful
eyes. 'Don't, O'Connor,' she said softly. 'That was a beautiful kiss. I won't let you regret it.'

He laughed without humour. 'I was out of line.'

'No, you weren't. You got there just before I did.'

He met her eyes, his startled, and then he chuckled. 'I
do believe you're telling the truth.'

'Oh, I am,' she said round a mouthful of prawns in
mayonnaise. 'I was beginning to think you'd never get
round to it without a little help.'

He choked on his first forkful of salad and Ginny
slapped him on the back and then eyed him as he swallowed and wiped his streaming eyes.

'Are you all right?'

'Fine,' he croaked. 'Just don't say things like that.'

'Like what? That I want you, too?'

He dropped his fork and pushed his plate away. 'Virginia, you're playing with fire here.'

'I certainly hope so.'

His eyes searched her face. 'I'm a widower,' he told her
bluntly. 'I've got two kids who take all my time and energy. This is going nowhere. It's just an affair.'

'That's fine,' she said. 'That's all I want too.'

She could see the tension in him escalate. He swallowed.
'There's no happy ever after, Ginny. Not for me. Not any
more.'

She wanted to cry for him, but she was all cried out for herself. 'That's fine,' she whispered. 'Where shall we go?'

'Now?' he said, his voice strangled.

'Why not?'

He stared at her for long seconds then, standing up, he pulled her to her feet. 'Friends of mine are away. They've given me the keys of their barn in case of emergencies. I think this qualifies.'

She laughed softly and followed him out of the sheltering cocoon. It seemed miles to the car, even further to the barn set high up on the side of a valley with a wood behind it and rolling fields in front.

They went in without a word, and upstairs to the only room that was furnished.

Then he turned to her, his eyes serious. 'Are you sure?' he murmured.

She nodded. 'Yes. Yes, I'm sure.'

His hands on her body were tender, almost reverent. He untied her blouse, spreading the sides and looking down at the full swell of her breasts under the skimpy T-shirt. 'So much woman,' he whispered.

Her breath caught as his hands slid under the hem of the T-shirt and cupped her breasts. They were naked under the soft cotton, ready for his touch, and he lifted the hem and brought his mouth to them in turn. She cried out, clinging to his shoulders, and he dragged her closer—his control ragged now—and buried his face in the side of her neck.

'This is probably going to be a disaster the first time, Virginia. It's been so damn long for me, but I'll make it up to you next time, I promise.' His lips pressed against the leaping pulse in the hollow of her throat and her head fell back, sensation swamping her.

He lowered her to the bed, bunching her skirt around

her waist, his hands finding and stripping away the tiny scrap of lace which was all she wore beneath the skirt.

His face was a mask now, taut with need and desire, and kneeling between her thighs he tore open his trousers with shaking hands and reached for her.

'Help me,' he muttered tightly. 'Virginia, help me—'

Then he was there, sliding home in the sweet nectar that her body wept for him, and tears welled in her eyes. She cradled him in her arms, her body arching to meet his, and he drove deeply into her—again and again and again— until with a harsh cry he shuddered against her and was still.

She was unfulfilled, but it didn't matter. He needed her, and she needed to be needed. OK, it was only physical and only fleeting, but she took what she could get.

The tears that filled her eyes overflowed and ran down into her hair, but she ignored them. Her attention was all on Ryan—his body slumped in her arms, his precious weight so welcome as he lay against her.

She felt the moment when he started to withdraw back into himself in a slight tension that invaded his shoulders. She let him go. There was no purpose to be served by trapping him against her.

She lay and watched as he swung away from her and fastened his clothes, then ran down the stairs and out into the fresh air.

She let him go. There would be time enough to talk to him. Mechanically she dried her tears and found her underwear, tugging it back on. He hadn't used a condom— probably hadn't even thought about it, she realised. Not that it mattered. She wasn't going to get pregnant as a result of his carelessness.

She tidied the bed and went downstairs. He was standing on a little terrace outside the French doors, staring out blindly across the valley. She left him to it, busying herself in the kitchen making coffee.

She took him a cup when it was done, putting it in his hand without a word.

He took it, looking surprised, and turned and met her eyes, his own remorseful. 'Virginia, I'm sorry. I behaved like an animal in there.'

'No, you didn't. You behaved like a man.'

'Was that as bitter as it sounded?'

She laughed without humour. 'It wasn't meant to be. Do you want to talk about it?'

He stared down the valley again, then started speaking. 'Ann died two years ago—nearly two and a half. There hasn't been anybody since—that was the first time.'

'And you feel guilty?'

He gave a grunt of laughter. 'I feel guilty because I didn't feel guilty—not about Ann, at least. I didn't give her a moment's thought. She was worth more than that, Virginia, and so are you.' He let out his breath on a shaky sigh and stared up at the heavens. 'I behaved appallingly.'

'No, you didn't—'

'I used you.'

Her heart contracted, and she closed her eyes against the tears and turned away. 'You had a good reason. Just don't do it again—not like that. Please?'

His hand on her shoulder was tender as he turned her into his arms, the soft sigh of regret as he saw her tears whispering over her skin like a caress.

'Forgive me,' he said unsteadily. 'I never meant to hurt you.'

She looked up and met his eyes. 'I forgive you. O'Connor?'

'Yes?'

'Make love to me.'

There was an endless pause and she held her breath, sure that he would turn and walk away—but he didn't. Slowly, softly, his mouth came down and covered hers, and he kissed her as he had done in the shelter of the willow tree.

They made love outside this time, under the night sky with the strange cries and rustlings of the night in the wood behind them, and their cries mingled with those of the animals and faded with the whispering breeze.

Then Ryan lifted his head and brushed the damp hair from her brow. 'OK?' he murmured.

She smiled, the damn tears threatening again in the safety of the darkness. 'Wonderful,' she lied.

Physically, it had been. Emotionally, though, it was a wasteland because she had committed the unpardonable folly of falling in love with him, and nothing would ever be quite the same again...

CHAPTER THREE

RYAN was swamped with emotion. Regret, remorse, excitement, passion, anticipation of their next meeting—but above all regret.

It was her tears that had done it. Those soft, cloud-grey eyes shimmering with disappointment—and that remark about him not behaving like an animal but like a man.

Was that what she expected from a lover? Disappointment? Haste? No finesse, no thought, no consideration?

She should be married with children of her own, he thought in confusion, not so desperate for affection that she would allow him access to her body with so little regard for her own physical and emotional well-being. His throat closed with a nameless emotion. Oh, Virginia, he thought. So tough, so worldly, so cool on the surface—and yet, deep down, so vulnerable and easily hurt.

Of all the girls to choose, he'd had to choose her. Still, the second time had been better. He'd made sure of that.

And the way she'd come apart in his arms—it was flattering, to say the least, and so easy to give her pleasure. A little more care and control the first time and he could have done it then—except that he couldn't have done.

He had to be realistic. The first time he had been totally out of control. She was just so lush, so soft, so feminine—all woman. After two and a half years he wasn't strong enough to hold on in the face of such exquisite temptation.

He lay in his bed alone, staring up at the ceiling and wondering what Ann would have thought of his behaviour. Their courtship had been slow and leisurely and humorous, and their love-making had never had the tempestuous quality he knew he would have with Virginia. Would Ann have understood the overwhelming urges he was feeling now?

Probably not. She had been soft and sweet and open, without a trace of guile. She would have been shocked, both at him and Virginia. Probably especially Virginia.

He was too, but he sensed that there was more to it than he understood. Beneath the bravado and sassy front she put on he felt a deep hurt—something too raw to talk about, too deep to probe and bring out into the cruel light of day.

Maybe one day she'd feel brave enough to tell him about it.

And that really tied in with a no-strings, sex-for-the-sake-of-it affair, O'Connor, he thought drily.

Oh, damn.

He rolled onto his front, smashed the pillow into submission and shut his eyes. He'd deal with it on Monday.

Ginny wasn't sure how to face Ryan on Monday morning. She was sure that her feelings for him were written all over her face in letters ten feet high, and she had no intention of revealing her stupidity to him. It was hardly his fault, after all, that she had managed to fall in love with the man.

She had a choice, of course. End the affair before she was hurt, or let it run its course. She was there for a year. Ryan had made it clear that he wanted no emotional involvement with her, so the choice was hers, really, so long as she could keep her feelings secret.

So, what was the choice? Hurt now, or have a lot of fun and hurt later? Some choice.

So she dressed for power, in a practical but ultra-feminine dress with a scooped neckline and button-through front, and had to spend the day fighting off all the conscious male patients between fifteen and eighty-five.

And Ryan.

He found her during a lull and called her into his office, and without preamble he pulled her into his arms and kissed her thoroughly. Then he buttoned her coat shut.

'It's too hot,' she protested, and one brow arched in comment.

'You don't say,' he drawled softly. 'That's why I did it up.'

She laughed, a little breathlessly, and his fingers cupped her jaw with infinite tenderness and he kissed her again.

'I want you,' he murmured.

'Mmm. Lunchtime?'

His eyes widened. 'Where?'

'My room?'

He looked tempted. 'There won't be time,' he said regretfully.

'Tonight?'

He shook his head and she was conscious of a hideous disappointment. 'I've got the kids to think about. I have to pick them up from their babysitter. Don't worry, we'll find time somehow—soon.'

His bleeper squawked and he picked up the phone, his eyes still on hers. 'O'Connor. Yes, I'm in the department. I'll come now.'

He put the phone down. 'Duty calls,' he said with a wry grin. 'Keep the coat done up.'

She grinned and let him go, then followed him out.

She did as he said for a while, but then it got too hot and she was too busy and the buttons gave way to comfort. By lunchtime the coat was off too, and she was wearing just the dress with her stethoscope round her neck.

Ryan walked past the cubicle where she was treating a

patient, stopped dead and reversed and looked pointedly at her chest.

She threw him a sassy grin and carried on, and as he walked away she could have sworn she heard a little growl erupting from his chest.

She stifled the chuckle and drew her attention back to her patient. 'Now, Mrs Robson, how did you say you cut yourself?'

He was right about lunchtime. They were rushed off their feet, and any plans they might have made to creep away for a quiet interlude would have been abandoned anyway.

Things were still fairly hectic when a woman was brought in who had fallen onto her outstretched hand and broken her arm. She was brought in in a wheelchair, obviously in a great deal of pain and suffering from shock.

Ginny examined her arm quickly and found that there was a very weak pulse in her wrist and the area over the back of her thumb felt dead.

That indicated damage to the nerve and blood supply down her arm, and would need surgical intervention. Ginny ordered an immediate X-ray, and as soon as the plate was in front of her she could see the damage caused by the fall. The humerus had split lengthwise in a nasty spiral fracture, and the sharp end of the lower part had rammed up into the nerves and blood vessels with the force of the fall. The woman would need an operation very quickly to sort out the blood supply and avoid potentially horrendous problems resulting from the disrupted circulation.

She called the orthopaedic registrar on take, and a few minutes later a good-looking young man appeared in the corridor.

'Who wants me?' he said with a grin, and the nurses ribbed him mercilessly.

'You're married, Zach, behave,' they teased.

The sister sent him in to Ginny, and she showed him the plate.

'Ow. That's quite a break. Is this your arm?' he said to the patient, squatting down to bring himself to her eye level.

'Yes—oh, it's so sore.'

'I'm sure. Don't worry. We'll have you sorted out in no time. When did you last eat?'

'Breakfast. I'm on a diet so I skipped lunch.'

'What about a drink? Can you remember when you had the last one?'

'About eleven o'clock. I was on my way home after doing the shopping when I fell off the bus.'

'Is that how you did this?' His fingers were gently examining her hand, which also showed signs of cuts and bruises. 'Poor you. That was a nasty fall. Let's get you up to Theatre, then, and sort you out. Any allergies or problems with anaesthetics?'

She shook her head, and Zach stood up.

'OK. Let's have her on a trolley, I think, and with that arm supported on a pillow like it is, and we'll get her fixed up as soon as Theatre's free—about ten minutes, Robert said.'

Ginny nodded. 'Do you want her up there for the anaesthetist now?'

'Yes, I think so. We'll get that pain sorted out first. I'll ring Theatre, if I may?'

'Of course.'

She filled in the paperwork while he went off to the office to phone, and then she put the notes on the trolley

with the patient and went along to the office to find out
what was happening.

Ryan was there, lounging in the doorway and chatting
to Zach.

'So, no emergencies over the weekend?' Zach said with
a grin. 'No fires or floods or burglars?'

Ryan looked a little uncomfortable. 'No, no emergencies. We went over there on Saturday evening and checked
it out.'

Ginny's eyes widened. Zach owned the barn? Oh, Lord.
She felt hot colour creeping up her neck, and turned
away so that Ryan didn't catch her eye because, as sure
as eggs, if he did she'd start to giggle.

She thought Zach would latch on to the 'we' like a
limpet, but he didn't, and Ginny realised that he must have
thought Ryan was referring to the children. She let her
breath ease out, and turned back again.

'Your patient's all ready for you, Zach,' she murmured,
and slipped away before she could become embroiled in
any further conversation about the barn.

Ryan came and found her a few minutes later. There
was a lull and she was in the staffroom with her feet up,
grabbing a cup of coffee. For the moment, at least, they
were alone.

He poured a cup of coffee and came and sat at right
angles to her, next to her feet.

'You could have told me the barn was his,' she said
softly. 'I nearly died.'

He chuckled. 'I didn't think of it. I forgot you'd meet
him around the department. Yes, it was a bit tricky, wasn't
it?'

'Would they mind?'

He shook his head. 'No—I'd just rather keep it more
discreet.'

Category Three again, she thought to herself. Oh, well, beggars couldn't be choosers.

'So,' he was saying, 'what are you doing this evening?'

'I thought you had to pick your children up?'

'I do. I meant later. You could come round.'

'To the house?'

'No. Bad idea, they might wake up.'

'You could get a babysitter.'

He swallowed and nodded. 'There's the problem of where we go,' he said quietly. 'Your hospital room is too public, Zach and Jilly are back, my house is out of the question and I'm just too old to mess about in parked cars.'

'I'll have to get a flat,' she said.

He snorted softly. 'That doesn't help us tonight, does it?'

'No. Not really.'

He grinned and stood up. 'I have an idea. Don't go away.'

He was gone for three minutes and came back with a wide smile. 'Jilly's flat's still vacant. It's just behind the hospital, very easy for you to get to work, it has a phone—and it's available now.'

'Now?'

'As of this minute. The hospital has it on a long lease. The accommodations officer will give you the keys.'

'Just like that?'

'Just like that.'

She was sceptical. 'What if I don't like it?'

'You'll like it,' he said confidently. 'It's a nice flat. It's even got a little garden.'

'So how come it's available?'

He grinned. 'Jilly handed the keys back this morning. She's been a bit forgetful—rather a lot on their minds.

They only got married two weeks ago.' His grin widened. 'Want a hand to move in tonight?'

'There's not a lot to move in,' she told him. 'Two suitcases, a box of books, a few bits and pieces. Certainly no furniture.'

'It's furnished.'

'Oh.'

'Well—go on, then, go and see the accommodations officer and get the keys. If you don't like it you can tell him so tomorrow.'

'What about work? I can't just walk out,' she protested.

He laughed. 'Who's going to tell the boss on you, Virginia?'

She smiled ruefully. 'OK, I'm going. Sure you can cope?'

'Oh, I'll find a way,' he said softly.

'Of course there are one or two things we didn't consider,' Ginny said later as they looked around the flat.

'Such as?'

'Sheets, towels, food—nothing important!'

He glanced at his watch. It was a quarter to eight. The supermarket might still be open if they hurried. 'I can lend you sheets and towels, and we can get food now,' he told her.

So they did a two-minute trolley dash in the supermarket, and then dropped by his house to pick up some linen. She sat in the car outside and looked around the neighbourhood at the neat little houses, all set back from the road with pretty front gardens and lots of trees and smart cars on the drives, and wondered how the frustrated sex fiend she had discovered in him fitted into suburbia.

They went back to the flat, but they didn't get very far. The shopping was put away—more or less—and the sheets were put on the bed, but only in a manner of speaking. Ginny put the pile down on the corner of the mattress and Ryan took her in his arms and looked down into her eyes and she caught fire again.

His mouth brushed hers, his lids fluttering down as sensation washed over them, and she closed her eyes and gave herself up to his kiss. He was hungry for her, she could tell, but he held back, slowing the pace deliberately—kissing her with lingering intent until her knees threatened to buckle.

Then he laid her down on the bed in amongst the folded blankets and tired pillows, and his fingers walked down her throat and stopped at the top button of her dress. 'I've been wanting to do this all day,' he murmured.

He slipped the first button free, pushed back the edge of her dress and kissed the pale swell of her breasts. Then the next button gave way, and the next, and with each one he kissed the skin he revealed.

She hardly dared to breathe as he reached her waist and started down her abdomen. What would he say? Would he be repulsed? It had been dark before and he'd been too blinded by urgency to notice trivia.

Sure enough, he paused, a frown pleating his brows. 'What happened?' he asked, his fingers tracing the savage network of scars that spanned the area between her hip-bones.

'I had a car accident when I was seventeen. I had internal injuries. We hit a bridge and the railings came through the bodywork.'

'Ouch.' His fingers were gentle. 'Poor baby.'

She closed her eyes as he bent and kissed the jagged lines. His fingers resumed their work with the buttons, her thighs and then her calves receiving his attention, and then he raised himself on one elbow and looked at her.

Her dress was gone, pushed aside in his slow exploration, and only her underwear remained. Her bra was front-fastening and, with his eyes fixed on hers, he slipped the catch and let her breasts spill into his waiting hands.

'So much woman,' he murmured, and she closed her eyes and bit down on the little cry that rose in her throat as his mouth fastened hotly over one nipple and suckled hard. She writhed under him, sensation ripping through her as he bit and sucked and licked and blew cold air over her sensitive skin, until she couldn't stand it any more.

Then, shedding her clothes, she knelt up on the bed and reached for his shirt buttons.

'Your turn,' she told him, and with slow deliberation she slipped each button in turn through its buttonhole, and when she reached his waistband she pulled the tails out and undid the last button, then pushed the shirt over his shoulders. He rolled over—shedding the sleeves one at a time—then rolled back, his eyes fixed hungrily on hers as she reached for the buckle of his belt.

The only sound in the room was the harsh rasp of his breath, and in the near-silence the scrape of the zip was almost deafening.

She caught her fingers in the waistband of his trousers and briefs, and he lifted his hips as she peeled the clothes away. As she reached his ankles he kicked his shoes off and lifted his feet, and she grabbed his socks in passing and pulled them off too.

Then he was naked, all hers, and she thought her heart would stop beating she wanted him so much. Emotion clawed at her—love, despair, emptiness, need—and when he reached for her she fell into his arms with a little sob and buried her face in his shoulder.

'Virginia?' he murmured, and the soft drawl was her undoing.

'Please, O'Connor,' she whimpered. 'Please…'

'Do I need to use anything? I forgot to ask the other night.'

'No, it's OK,' she said. 'O'Connor, please—'

'You're sure? I'd hate to get you pregnant.'

Her heart splintered in her chest. 'I'm sure,' she whispered rawly. Her eyes closed over the tears that she wouldn't shed. He'd never promised her happy ever after, so what was the point of grieving for what she could never have?

She concentrated on what she could have—the feel of his body on hers, in hers; and as his mouth found hers and fastened on it he started to move, slowly at first and then faster, and she matched his rhythm and reached the pinnacle with him, her body contracting around his as he spilled deep within her.

And if the cry that was torn from her wasn't one of ecstasy but of pain, he was unaware. Only Ginny knew, and she smiled through her tears and kissed him back and hid the anguish as she had so many times before…

It was a lovely little flat, she discovered after Ryan had gone and she'd had time to explore it sensibly.

The entrance to the flat was off the main hall, near the front door, and there was an inner hall leading to the living-room and kitchen. The bedroom was at the front, accessed from the living-room which had a tired but comfortable three-piece suite and a casement door out into the walled garden. It was more of a yard, really, with a gravelled area and a few beds and some pots and tubs, the contents of which looked a little the worse for wear. Still, it was a little oasis and with a bit of effort would be lovely. Much better than her little room at the hospital.

The kitchen had a door out to the garden too, and there

was a bench seat with a late honeysuckle tangling over the wall above it and scenting the night air with a sweet perfume that spoke of love and stolen moments. She made a cup of coffee and took it outside, sitting on the bench and resting her head back against the wall and thinking about Ryan.

He had gone back to his children, back to his duties and responsibilities and the world that he belonged to and from which she would always be excluded.

'I love you,' she whispered to the night air, and a cat came out of nowhere and helped itself to her lap, and she stroked it and rubbed its ears and was grateful for the company. Perhaps she should get a cat—or perhaps she just had.

'Where do you live, puss?' she asked him, but he just kneaded her thigh and dribbled and didn't answer. Oh, well, either he'd stay or he'd go. Perhaps Jilly Samuels knew about him. She'd have to ask Zach the next time she saw him.

Her flat was wonderful, she decided the following morning. She'd slept well all night, despite the emotional turmoil Ryan's touch had caused in her. It was quieter than her hospital room and, although the bed wasn't as new, the bedroom was so much bigger that it seemed a small price to pay—and in addition there was the living-room, the kitchen and the garden.

It only took her three minutes longer to get to the department as well, and she found that a big plus. It was one of the reasons she hadn't looked for a flat in the first place—because she had to be based at the hospital when she was on call. This way, although she could sleep in the department during the night when she was duty, she could

slip home to change or eat something and still be in range
of her bleeper.

It was an excellent arrangement, she decided, sharing
her bench with the cat while she ate her breakfast. Truly
excellent—and if the reasons for her taking the flat in the
first place didn't really bear close inspection it was, nev-
ertheless, a very sound move.

Yes. She liked it enormously, and the cat seemed
pleased too. He was climbing onto her lap and sticking his
face in her toast before she realised what he was up to.

'You're a cheeky beast,' she scolded lovingly, pushing
him away. 'Go on.'

He subsided reluctantly, watching every bite, and she
weakened and gave him the last morsel. He didn't eat the
toast, of course—just licked the butter off it. 'Fussy cat,'
she said affectionately, and when she got to work she rang
the orthopaedic ward where Zach's wife was one of the
nurses.

'Oh, yes, the cat,' Jill said brightly. 'He's lovely—a bit
domineering, but very friendly. Watch the butter—he'll
lick it if you leave it out on the table. And he likes sponge
cake, and he's a terror for chicken or raw steak. He lives
over the wall at the bottom with an old lady, and she spoils
him rotten. So, what do you think of the flat?'

'It's lovely,' Ginny told her. 'What fortuitous timing.'

'Mmm—wasn't it? They go very fast around here—you
were lucky to get it. Well, I hope you get on OK. Anything
else you want to know, just ask.'

She promised to do just that, and as she put the phone
down the direct line from Ambulance Control started to
ring.

'Got a burns case coming in, love,' the controller told
her. 'Domestic incident—house fire. Middle-aged man
asleep upstairs—just come off night duty. Cause of fire

unknown but heavy fumes reported so stand by for respiratory burns and cyanide poisoning, also extensive burns over the face and head. You might get a couple of the firemen, too, with smoke inhalation.'

'Thank you. I'll alert everyone here,' she told him, and went to find Ryan.

'Burns coming in,' she told him, and repeated what she'd been told.

'Right. Let's alert Cambridge to expect him after he's stabilised and get ready for him. If there was smoke and he's got facial burns we'll need an anaesthetist to put in an airway and monitor him. We'll need to check his blood for carbon monoxide or cyanide poisoning because of the fumes, and we'll need to get fluids into him and some one hundred per cent oxygen and nebulised salbutamol if he's wheezing.'

She nodded. 'Shall I alert the nursing staff after I call for an anaesthetist?'

'Please. I'll go and make sure Resus is ready with the things I want—send the senior nursing staff in; they can give me a hand.'

They were just ready as the ambulance arrived, and the team went smoothly into action. The first job was to cool the burns down and establish an airway, and the anaesthetist arrived then to do so. It was a struggle because the burns around the man's face were full thickness, and the skin was stiff and unyielding, leathery and without any feeling. At least they didn't hurt him, Ginny thought, horrified by the extent of his burns.

His hands were bad too, the fingers especially beginning to swell, and Jack Lawrence—who had trained as a surgeon—came in and slit the skin on each of the patient's fingers, the inside of his upper arm and around his neck to relieve the constriction and protect the underlying tissues from compression. He didn't need an anaesthetic. In all of those areas the skin was quite dead, the nerves destroyed.

The man's breathing was rough and wheezy, his lungs obviously compromised, and she saw Jack and Ryan exchange a significant glance across his body. Jack shook his head, and Ryan nodded.

So they didn't give him much chance, then. She concentrated her efforts on getting an intravenous line in with a large-bore cannula. His arms were hopeless, and his circulation was so depressed that she didn't think she'd manage in his leg either.

'I think I need to do a cut-down to get this line in,' she told Ryan.

'Fine. Go ahead. Are you happy to do it?'

She was happier doing that than she was up at the head end, anyway, she thought, and in fact it was quite easy. She gave him a local anaesthetic, but she wasn't convinced that he was conscious. Certainly as soon as she got a line in he'd be more comfortable because he could have morphine to dull the pain in the peripheral areas where the burns were less severe.

He was moaning now, and Ryan was talking to him. 'Can you hear me, Dennis?' he was saying. 'You're in hospital now, you're all right. Try and relax—don't fight the tube. Is that line in yet?'

'Almost—yes, it's there.'

'Right, get some morphine in—three milligrammes— then get the fluid in.'

A nurse handed her a syringe of morphine, she checked it and injected it slowly into the cannula. Dennis stopped moaning, but he was still restless which, she knew, could be lack of oxygen due to the burns in his lungs or dehydration. 'How much fluid?' she asked Ryan.

'He's got approximately twenty to twenty-five per cent burns, mostly partial thickness but quite extensive full thickness around the face and neck—I would say go for twenty-five per cent, multiplied by his weight in kilos and divided by two.'

She looked at the patient. 'What does he weigh—eighty kilos?'

'I would say about that.'

She did a rapid calculation in her head. 'So he needs—one thousand. A litre an hour?'

'No—four hours. Four hours from the time of the burn—so a thousand millilitres in the next three hours, a thousand in the four hours after that and a thousand in the four after that.'

'Right. Normal saline?'

'Haemaccel first, then saline. And he'd better have an antiemetic after that morphine or he'll start to throw up.'

Again the nurse was ready with it, and she injected the drug into his thigh muscle.

'What now?'

'Saline dressings over that face and neck, and over his hands, and let's get him moved on to Cambridge to the burns unit. Everybody happy that he's stable?'

'The ambulance is standing by,' a nurse said. 'We've alerted Cambridge. They're waiting for your instructions.'

'Good. Right, someone had better go with him, I suppose.'

He looked up at them all, and grinned. 'I get to be the lucky one, do I? OK. Can you deal with the firemen?'

'Just go,' Jack said drily. 'Even you aren't indispensable.'

He was gone three hours, and he came back with the news that the man had arrested just as they reached the outskirts of Cambridge and it was touch and go whether he would survive.

Ginny wasn't surprised. He had looked very seriously ill, and the invisible damage to his lungs was probably more significant than the damage to his skin. At least that could be grafted. The firemen were both all right, discharged after examination and blood tests for cyanide and carbon monoxide poisoning and with minor burns to their hands treated, not for the first time judging by the scarring.

They carried on with their work, and at four fifteen a call came from Cambridge to say that they had lost Dennis. His lungs had been unable to cope after the smoke and heat, and his heart had given up with the strain. Despite all their efforts, they had been unable to resuscitate him.

Ginny found herself unaccountably relieved, in a way. Had he survived he would have been hideously scarred and would have had to endure a very protracted and painful recovery, with countless skin grafts and other operations on contractures in his hands, for instance.

Even so, it left them all feeling deflated and she wasn't surprised when Ryan didn't come round that evening.

She had the flat to herself, which gave her an opportunity to unpack and sort the place out and also bring over the last few things from her room in the hospital. She needed a few pictures, she decided—nothing expensive, just some prints from an art shop she'd seen in town at the weekend. One in the sitting-room over that rather hideous fireplace, and one in the bedroom. Maybe more.

The cat came and sat on her bed and watched her put her clothes away and, having decided that she was very boring, he curled up in a ball and went to sleep.

'I hope you haven't got fleas,' she said repressively.

He flicked an ear back, but apart from that treated her remark with the contempt it deserved.

She finished her unpacking without the benefit of his company, but he reappeared when she made some toast and took the butter out of the fridge.

'You again,' she said with no great rancour, and he purred and flung himself against her legs, arching his back and commanding her to stroke him.

'Soppy date. Go on, go home, your owner will be worried about you.'

She pushed him out of the door and shut it, and tried to ignore the pitiful mewing. He was far from pitiful, she told herself. He was just a nuisance. She let him in anyway, and he sat on her lap and watched the little portable television she had had in her room. Then at ten o'clock she heard a feeble voice calling, 'Geronimo? Come on, son.'

He stood up and arched his back, flexed his claws on her knee and jumped down, miaowing at the door. 'Is that you, mush?' she asked him. 'Are you Geronimo?'

He squawked at her, and she let him out and watched as he ran down the garden, leapt up and walked along the wall then disappeared.

'There you are, you bad boy,' the quavering voice said. 'Have you been making a nuisance of yourself? Come on, then, time for your supper.'

She heard a door shut and, smiling, returned to her seat. Geronimo, eh? Well, he sounded much loved—maybe because out of respect for his elderly owner he didn't strop his claws in her leg!

CHAPTER FOUR

GINNY heard the child coming even before the doors of the department were opened. Triage be damned, she thought. She'd just finished a patient.

She went out to the front of the department in time to see a staff nurse take the mother by the arm and lead her into the triage room, the screaming baby in her arms.

'OK, Fran, I'll deal with it,' she said. 'Can you come and take the details while I look at the baby?'

The mother looked up at her gratefully, her eyes panic-stricken. 'She just won't stop screaming. She's all right for a while, but then she starts to scream and scream and I can't do anything to help her—' The tears were more imminent now, and Ginny put her arm round the woman's shoulders and comforted her briefly.

'Come with me. Let's see if we can sort it out,' she said reassuringly.

As they walked she ran through her paediatric reference book in her head. Pallor, intermittent screaming—

'Has she vomited at all?'

'Yes. Twice now—when she has the screaming fits.'

Just then the baby retched again and the screaming resumed even more loudly.

'Poor little love. Put her on the couch and let me look at her, could you?'

They prised the child's arms away from her mother's neck, and as Ginny stripped her she asked questions.

'How old is she?'

'Fifteen months. Nearly sixteen.'

'Any trouble before?'

'No. Colic when she was tiny sometimes, but nothing like this.'

'Right. When did it start?'

'This morning—about eight o'clock. I had to get the others to school and she seemed better, then she did it again at ten to nine and then now so I brought her straight here. I thought she must have appendicitis.'

Ginny looked at her watch. A quarter to ten. She gently felt the abdomen and found a soft mass on the right hand side. 'No, I don't think so. I want to do a rectal examination. I don't suppose she'll like it. Will you hold her for me on the couch?'

She put gloves on, lubricated her little finger and gently examined the baby's rectum. She screamed and wriggled, and when Ginny withdrew her finger it had what looked like redcurrant jelly on it. She stripped off her gloves.

'Right. I want abdominal X-rays—standing and lying down, please—and I want a paediatric surgeon called. I think she might have a little section of bowel turned inside out, in which case she'll need an operation to sort it out—and the quicker the better because she isn't enjoying this, poor little love.'

She stroked the baby's head tenderly. 'Sorry, my darling. I didn't mean to hurt you. Hush, now.'

The staff nurse took the X-ray request and the baby round to the radiographer while Ginny got all the details of name and address and previous history, and filled in the mother on the potential treatment. She was understandably worried sick, but Ginny did her best to reassure her that the baby would be all right in the end.

As soon as the baby was back Ginny set up an intravenous line, took blood for testing and started a slow drip of saline to rehydrate her young patient, then Ross Hamilton came down and examined the little one, checked her X-rays and confirmed the diagnosis.

'So, what happens now?' the mother asked, trying to be calm.

'Well, we'll have to admit her to the children's ward straight away,' Ross said. 'It's possible we may be able to turn this bowel the right way out with a barium enema, which could push the loop out the other way and straighten it out. That would save her undergoing surgery and is obviously preferable, but we can't guarantee it will work. We'll try, though—and, whatever happens, she should make a perfectly good recovery.'

He turned to Ginny. 'If you could make arrangements for the baby's admission I'll go and get things ready for the barium enema.'

He left them, and Ginny sent the mother and child off with a porter to the ward, armed with the notes and a sick bowl—just in case. She watched them go, the baby quiet now as her bowel had obviously entered a resting phase, and as she turned back she found Ryan watching her.

'Problems?' he said softly.

'Intussusception. Ross Hamilton is going to try and reduce it with a barium enema.'

'Poor baby.'

'Mmm.' She turned back to her cubicle and picked up her pen off the desk, fiddling with the spring. Her arms felt empty, her heart also. What was it like to hold your own child in your arms?

'Virginia?'

She swallowed and lifted her head. 'Yes?'

'Are you OK?'

'Mmm. Just a bit busy.'

It was an obvious lie. She slipped the pen into her breast pocket, leaving a streak of blue down the front of her white coat, and turned back, throwing him a smile. 'Are you coming over later?'

His eyes searched her face and she felt distinctly uncomfortable. What would he see? Longing? Regret?

Love?

'Yes,' he said eventually. 'About eight-thirty?'

She nodded. 'Supper?'

'Sounds good.'

She pasted a smile on for him and patted his cheek as she went past. 'Don't count your chickens. I'm not the world's best cook.'

'Honey, you'd have to go some to be worse than me,' he murmured, catching her hand.

'Put me down, O'Connor,' she said mildly. 'You don't know where I've been.'

No. He didn't. He had no idea what private hell she'd come from, but something was burning a hole in her the size of Alaska, and he badly wanted to know what it was.

He'd seen her with the baby, her hands gentle, her face concerned. She should be married, he thought again. Maybe she had been. He'd never even asked her, but they both avoided personal conversation. Of course, for the purposes of their businesslike affair it was irrelevant.

He sighed shortly. Damn.

He didn't *want* to care...

She'd lied. She was a good cook. It was a shame he was in no mood to do it justice.

He'd walked through her front door with strict instructions to himself not to jump her bones the second he crossed the threshold. As a result, he was making polite conversation and admiring her cooking when all he could think about was taking her in his arms and losing himself in that wonderful feminine body.

So much woman.

Damn. He burnt his tongue on a potato and swallowed it, scorching his throat all the way down. He reached for a glass of water and caught it with his fingers, sending it all over her.

She leapt up with a little shriek, throwing her chair over backwards and narrowly missing the cat—who shot out through the open door and took himself off. Ryan stood up and went round to her, dabbing ineffectually at her wringing wet skirt with a paper napkin.

'I'm soaked,' she told him unnecessarily.

'Mmm. Better get you out of that before you catch your death of cold.'

It was a chokingly hot August evening, but they both ignored the absurdity of his remark.

'Good idea,' she murmured.

And that was the end of their meal.

Ginny lay awake and watched him as he slept, his skin gilded by the soft glow of the bedside light. It threw his face into relief, and she could see the shadow of stubble on his jaw. She would have whisker burns on her body tomorrow, she thought lazily, all over her breasts where he had lavished so much attention.

He was a wonderful lover, gentle, considerate, patient— not that he needed to be very patient. She was so in tune with him, so ready for him that she'd come apart at the seams tonight as soon as he'd touched her, then again when his own body had clamoured for release.

She smoothed his hair back from his forehead and gazed longingly at him. It was such a shame that things were as they were, and that they would never be together as they could have been.

Her arms still felt empty. Holding that baby had done

something to her insides; triggered a basic instinct that she could usually ignore, but tonight for some reason it was screaming at her. Because he was there? Because their love-making was just a sham, never destined to fulfil its purpose and create a life that was a little part of both of them?

A lump rose in her throat and, bending over, she kissed him lightly on the lips.

His eyes fluttered open and he smiled lazily at her. 'Hi there,' he said gruffly, his voice rough with sleep.

'Hi. You need to go—it's getting late.'

He glanced at his watch and groaned, then threw off the quilt and stood up, rummaging for his things in the tangle of discarded clothes they had abandoned in their haste by the side of the bed. He held up his trousers, crumpled and damp from her skirt, and pulled a rueful face.

'I really look as if I've been to a meeting,' he said drily.

'Say someone knocked a glass of water over. It's the truth.'

'It's just another half-truth,' he said disgustedly, and fear rose like bile in her throat. Was it all getting too much for him—the lies, the sneaking around?

They didn't have to, she reminded herself. He could always come out into the open and admit that he was having an affair, but Ann's mother looked after the children and he seemed very reluctant for her to know that there was another woman in his life now.

Why? Did she expect her son-in-law to live like a monk?

Maybe he was the one with the problem. Perhaps he really did feel guilty facing up to his needs.

Was that why he kept her out of his life? Was the house just a shrine to Ann?

It seemed that she would never know because he was

always most insistent that they met only at her flat and after the children were asleep. She wondered if she would ever meet them—and then decided that if she was going to react so strongly to a stranger's baby then meeting Ryan's children would be the last straw.

No. It was better like this. A little distance was no bad thing.

He turned and bent over, kissing her softly on the lips. 'Night, Virginia. Sleep tight.'

'And you, O'Connor. Drive carefully.'

'I will. I always do.'

She watched him go, pulling the curtain aside so that she could see him as he crossed the street to his car. He turned and waved, then slid behind the wheel, started the engine and pulled quietly away.

She dropped the curtain and looked round the bedroom. What a mess.

It went well with her life.

Despite their best efforts at keeping their affair quiet, inevitably it didn't remain a secret for long.

Patrick Haddon walked in on a stolen kiss one day and apologised, but there was a twinkle in his eyes and no great remorse. And, as if that wasn't bad enough, they were in her kitchen one evening later that same week, her blouse undone and his shirt pulled out of his trousers—all but making love where they stood—when the doorbell rang.

Ryan leapt away from her as if he'd been burnt. 'Who the hell is that?' he muttered, stabbing his hands through his hair and ramming his shirt back in his trousers.

She scrabbled for the front of her blouse. 'I have no idea. Probably some obscure religious sect. Stay here; I'll tell them to go away.'

She smoothed her hair back, took a deep breath and

opened the door to the lobby. There in the hall, by the open front door and in full view of Ryan, were Zach and a woman Ginny had never met before.

Their eyes flicked past her to Ryan, then back to her, then to each other.

'Sorry,' Zach said, and cleared his throat, obviously embarrassed to have caught them so nearly *in flagrante delicto*. 'We didn't mean to—er—interrupt. We just popped in to see if everything was all right with the flat.'

Ginny gave a mental shrug. She had nothing to hide. She stepped back and opened the door wider, giving them a wry smile. 'Come in. I take it you're Jilly?'

The woman nodded and held out her hand. 'Hi. Nice to meet you at last.' She released her hand and went to Ryan, giving him a hug. 'Hi there, you old reprobate. You've been neglecting us recently.'

Ryan flushed but returned her hug. 'Hello, Jilly. I'm sorry, I didn't mean to neglect you. Things have been kind of hectic.'

'So I see,' she said drily. 'You are a dark horse.'

He closed his eyes and gave a rueful snort. 'Oh, hell, you might as well know—everyone else seems to be finding out about us.'

'Why the big secret, anyway?' Zach asked bluntly. 'It's high time there was a woman in your life.'

'I have a woman in my life,' he muttered. 'My mother-in-law. She wouldn't approve.'

'And what's it got to do with her?'

He thrust his hands through his hair and sighed. 'Nothing, I suppose, except that I'm very dependent on her goodwill for help with the children, and I don't want the kids upset or hurt by people talking.'

'Saying what?' Jilly demanded. ' "Finally Ryan

O'Connor has stopped living like a monk''? Ryan, you have a right to a life of your own!'

'I know that,' he sighed. 'It's just hard to balance everything without hurting the people that deserve it the least.'

'It's OK,' Ginny said quietly. 'I understand. We'll work it out. Anyway, there are other reasons for keeping it quiet. We have to work together—'

Zach snorted. 'And you think people won't notice? Dream on, lady. This is a hospital. You can't sneeze without a running commentary.'

She laughed. 'I had noticed. I've only been there three and a half weeks and I know the ins and outs of everybody's love lives—and, believe me, I didn't ask!' She reached for the kettle. 'Coffee?'

'Lovely. So, enough about your private life. How's the flat?'

'Wonderful. Very handy for work, and a real retreat.'

'How's the cat?'

'A thief. I left some bacon out yesterday.'

'Oops!'

They swapped a smile, and Ginny decided she liked the other woman—despite her willowy figure and fabulous blonde hair. She plugged the kettle in and turned back to face them all.

Zach's eyes zeroed in on her bust. 'Um—forgive me for being familiar, but are your buttons meant to work like that?'

She looked down, and hot colour flooded her cheeks. 'Oh, hell. That's his fault.'

Zach laughed. 'I don't doubt it. You should have just told us to go.'

'What—like you two did when I caught you in the shower?'

It was Jilly's turn to blush but Zach just grinned, quite unabashed. 'Actually, as you were in on that moment, you may as well hear our news. We're having a baby—and it was conceived in the shower on that very occasion.'

Ryan laughed, clearly delighted by their news and amused by the connection. For Ginny, though, it was another arrow to her heart. Under cover of Ryan's congratulations and hugs, she made the coffee and pulled herself together. So what if they were having a baby? People did it all the time.

Other people. Not her.

Never her.

Still, Ryan didn't want more than a simple affair, and at this time in her life her career had to take precedence anyway.

It didn't stop her hurting.

That evening seemed to mark a turning point in their relationship. Maybe it was something Zach said, or maybe Ryan had been getting round to it anyway, but on Friday he asked her if she was busy the next day.

'Jilly and Zach have gone away for the weekend and I've got their dog—well, Zach's sister's dog, but she's got a young child and he's not very well, and she's finding the dog a bit much, so they said they'd have him back. Anyway, I've got him for the weekend and the kids and I were going to take him for a walk and take a picnic lunch and just spend the day mooching around in the forest somewhere—I just wondered if you'd like to join us?'

So she would meet his children after all. She dredged up a brave smile. 'That sounds lovely. Thank you.'

In fact, she found herself dreading it. Saturday dawned bright and clear, another cloudless, scorching hot day, and she wore jeans and a little vest-top and that gauzy blouse tied under the bust again to keep the sun off her shoulders.

He picked her up at ten, and as he settled her in the car she turned round and got her first sight of the children.

She would have known them anywhere. The spitting image of their father, they were bright-eyed and bushy-tailed and clearly excited. So, too, was the dog. Huge, black and grinning, he leered over the back seat at her and woofed, almost lifting the car roof.

'Thank you, Scud, that'll do,' Ryan said ruefully. The dog sat, and she could hear his tail swishing and the children giggling as they set off. They drove for about twenty minutes, then Ryan pulled off the road into a picnic area on the edge of some heathland and parked the car in the shade of a group of pines.

'OK, troops, out you get,' he said cheerfully, and the children scrambled out of the car and rushed round to the back. Ryan handed each of them a colourful little rucksack, and then hoisted a much larger one onto his back.

'They've got their sandwiches,' he explained. 'I've got all the rest of the picnic, the drinks, the dog's water, a blanket—' He shrugged and grinned. 'That's what dads are for, isn't it? Hey, Scud, here, boy!'

They set off, walking through a track over the heather, and the sun beat down and scorched them. She was glad she'd thought of wearing her blouse because her skin would have burned to a frazzle by lunchtime otherwise. Ryan dolloped sunscreen on his children's skin before they had gone far, and at eleven o'clock she smeared some over his nose.

They were standing toe to toe while she put it on and his eyes were burning down at her, hotter than the sun.

'You've got that blouse on again,' he murmured.

'Mmm.'

'It does terrible things to my heart rate.'

'Hold still. It's good for you—cardiovascular exercise.'

'Are you talking dirty again?'

She chuckled and wiped her fingers down inside the open V of his shirt. 'You should be so lucky,' she teased.

Their eyes locked and sizzled, and then just as he was bending his head a little voice piped up, 'Are you going to kiss her?'

He jerked up straight and looked down. 'No, Evie. She was just putting suncream on my nose.'

'That was ages ago.'

'I was just making sure it was properly rubbed in,' Ginny said with great authority, 'and it is, so we can carry on now. Turn round and I'll put it away in the rucksack.'

'You can see why I daren't do much in front of them,' he murmured quietly as they followed the children down the track. 'Self-appointed guard dogs.'

'They're lovely children,' she said wistfully. 'They're just curious about me, and they love you. They're a credit to you.'

He stopped, and she stopped too and turned towards him. 'What is it?'

'Thank you,' he whispered, his voice rough.

'Well, they are,' she said frankly. 'They're lovely kids. It can't be easy, struggling to bring them up alone.'

He sighed. 'It isn't. It can be very hard. Sometimes I think it's too hard; it can't have been meant to be so difficult. Things go wrong, I'm late to pick them up or my schedule changes at the last minute—you can see why I have to rely on Ann's mother so much. We moved here after Ann died to be near them, just because they're the children's only relatives on their mother's side and I didn't want them to lose touch with her. I felt it was very important that they knew Ann was loved and that they were with people who could talk about her to them. Kids need that when they lose a parent.'

'So you didn't have your house when Ann was still alive?'

'No. I only bought it about eighteen months ago. We used to live in Sussex—I worked in Brighton.'

Ginny chewed her lip for a moment, then glanced across at him. 'How did she die?' she asked softly.

'Oh.' He shrugged. 'A car accident. A meaningless stupid accident that shouldn't have happened. I'd been on night duty, we were on our way up here for the weekend. Ann said she'd drive. We left the motorway and came off at a roundabout which was controlled by traffic lights at peak times. This car came at us from the right without any warning—he can't have seen the traffic lights. I'd just woken up and turned towards her, and the car came straight into her door without even braking. She died instantly. I know that—because she was flung across onto my lap and her head was caved in and her chest was crushed.'

Ginny closed her eyes and stumbled, and felt Ryan's hands fasten on her shoulders and steady her. She sagged against his chest, dragging in a lungful of air.

'How did you survive?' she asked.

His hand smoothed her hair. 'It was better than watching her suffer. The kids were both knocked out, so they didn't see her. I managed to get them both out of the car and away before they came round and realised what had happened. The rest of us were all quite unharmed—they were a little concussed, we all had the odd bruise, but nothing to speak of. Ann took it all—for all of us.'

His chest lifted, as if he was sucking in a much-needed lungful of air, and she tipped her head back and looked into his face.

He was miles away, his eyes clouded with the memories. She cupped his cheek with her hand. 'O'Connor? I'm sorry. I didn't mean to bring it all back.'

His hand covered hers and squeezed it gently. 'That's OK, honey, it's not your fault. It's time I told you, anyway. It's just a rather vivid picture, that's all.' He turned back towards the path. 'Come on, we need to catch up. The kids have disappeared.'

He set off down the track after the children, and she followed him a little more slowly, trying to absorb the horror of what he had told her. Imagine the woman you loved being flung onto your lap, so horribly injured. How on earth did a man deal with that? How could anybody deal with it? No wonder he was taking things slowly getting back into the mainstream of life.

She caught up with them sitting on a fallen tree, laughing together and throwing sticks for Scud, and they looked up and waved and she felt the emptiness inside shrink a little—as if their cheerfulness could fill the space with happiness.

She fished out a smile and went up to them. 'Tea-break?' she said hopefully.

Ryan grinned and pulled a bottle of cola out of the ruck-sack. 'Was that a hint?' He lobbed her the bottle and she caught it, but when she twisted the cap it spluttered all over her chest. Ryan leapt to his feet and dabbed at her with a handkerchief, mischief dancing in his eyes.

'I do believe you did that on purpose,' he murmured for her ears alone.

'Of course,' she said sassily, her grin wicked and sexy.

There was no lingering trace of sadness in his eyes, no remnant of grief lurking there to make her feel guilty for ruining his day. How well he covered his emotions, she thought sadly. She stilled his blotting hand.

'You'll wear out my blouse,' she told him gently.

His hand dropped and he searched her eyes. 'It's OK, Virginia,' he murmured, as if he knew what she was thinking. 'Really. Now, are you going to drink that stuff or just shake it up and spray it on everyone?'

She pursed her lips, hesitating—a wicked smile lurking in her eyes—and then with a quick twist she removed the lid, closed her lips round the top and tipped the bottle. He took it from her, his eyes locked with hers, and drank from it without wiping the top.

His message was sensuous, erotic and unequivocal.

It worked. She forgot Ann, forgot the children, forgot everything except the man standing in front of her.

He took the bottle top from her nerveless fingers, winked and turned back to the kids. 'You guys want a drink now?'

'Yes, please.'

'I don't want cola, I want orange,' Gus said.

'I know that. I've got your orange in here.'

He set the rucksack down and rummaged in it, coming up with a small bottle of orange juice. He handed it to his son, twisted off the cap and held it while the little boy drank then recapped it and put it back.

How many men would have remembered or bothered with a little boy's preferences?

'You finished, Evie?'

She nodded and handed him the bigger bottle, screwing the lid on as she did so, and he tightened it automatically before stashing it back in the bag. Then he swung it up onto his shoulders and held out his hands to the children. 'Come on, then, let's go and find a place to have lunch. Do you suppose we can find a river?'

They yomped along for another hour then, miraculously, there in front of them was a little stream bordered by trees, with a patch of grass in dappled sunlight where they could sit and have their picnic.

'Well, how about that?' Ryan said, winking at Ginny over their heads. 'A perfect place for lunch.'

'Handy little spot—have you been here before?' she asked with a smile while the children were organising their sandwiches.

He grinned at her. 'No—but Patrick comes here quite often with Anna and Flissy and the baby. He told me about it yesterday.'

'So, it wasn't exactly a surprise?'

He chuckled. 'Not exactly, no, but the kids enjoy it more if they think we've discovered it together.'

They ate their sandwiches, and then Ryan and the children rolled up their trouser legs and splashed about in the stream. 'Come join us,' Ryan called.

She was tempted, but her jeans wouldn't roll very far. Still, she took off her shoes and socks and waded in up to her ankles. It was blissfully cool, and it would have been fine if Ryan hadn't started the water fight...

'I'm sorry you got so wet,' he murmured when he dropped her off later.

'I'm fine. Just a bit soggy and wrinkled.'

'Let me help you out of those wet things,' he said, and she noticed the twinkle in his eye.

'Your children are in the car,' she reminded him.

He grinned. 'So wait for me. I'll be back at eight.'

'I'll turn into a prune.'

'So change now, quickly, and come back to the house with us for a barbecue.'

It sounded very tempting, but she thought it was pushing things. 'Whatever happened to Category Three?' she murmured.

'What?'

She laughed. 'Category Three—not work, not home, but the other one. That's where I fit, isn't it?'

His smile was like quicksilver, a little sad, gone almost before it had begun. 'Is that what you think? I have a separate category for you?'

'Don't you?'

He shook his head. 'No. Not any more. Zach's right, I have a right to a life. Please—change and come with us.'

She compromised. 'I'll follow you. You go now, and I'll change and come over in an hour or so. OK?'

He nodded and, turning on his heel, he ran back to the car. The children waved as they drove off, and she went in and spent half an hour in the bath trying to get the blue dye out of her legs from the jeans.

It was a good job his car seats were dark blue-grey and not a pale fawn, she thought as she scrubbed.

It was a hopeless task. She covered them with a long wispy skirt and a loose T-shirt, knotted a sweatshirt round her neck in case it got colder and drove to his house.

As she got out another car pulled up and an elderly couple emerged.

Ryan opened the door, looked from her to them and gave her a meaningful look. She took a steadying breath. If they were who she thought they were, all hell was about to break loose.

Evie and Gus shot out of the front door around Ryan and ran towards the couple. 'Granny, Grandpa! We went for a picnic with Ginny and Scud! It was excellent!'

'Ginny?'

The woman looked at her, and she looked back. She had done nothing to be ashamed of, and she wouldn't be made to feel like an intruder.

'Hello there,' she said with a smile.

Ryan cleared his throat. 'Virginia, I'd like you to meet Betty and Doug Powers, Ann's parents. Betty, Doug, this is Virginia.'

CHAPTER FIVE

VIRGINIA who? she could hear them thinking as Ryan invited them into the house. Who is she? What's she doing here with our daughter's husband? With our grandchildren?

Betty Powers put the questions into words, in a way. 'How nice to meet you,' she said politely, but her eyes were busily assessing, searching for a reason for Ginny's presence, looking for clues. 'Have you known Ryan long?' she added with apparent casualness.

'About four weeks now,' Ginny said, indulging the woman because she had, after all, got a vested interest in the situation in the form of her grandchildren. 'Since I started at the hospital. I'm his new SHO.'

'A colleague,' Betty said, tidying Ginny up into a safe slot.

Ryan could have left it at that, but he didn't. 'More than a colleague, Betty,' he said gently. 'Virginia and I are...' there was an eloquent pause '...friends. Close friends.'

Betty and Doug exchanged a quick glance, and Betty blushed and backed off a little. There was a distinct chill in the air after that, and the children did nothing to alleviate it because all they could talk about was how Ryan had splashed her in the river and she had pushed him over and sat on him and held his head under the water, and when he'd come up he had chased her all through the forest.

'He said she'd win a wet T-shirt competition,' Gus said guilelessly. 'Granny, what's a wet T-shirt competition?'

'To see who's got the wettest T-shirt, of course,' Evie said scornfully, while Ginny flushed scarlet and Ryan almost choked on his drink. There was a gasp of horror from Betty, Doug coughed in embarrassment and Ginny wondered why God wouldn't play fair and let a hole open up and swallow her.

The Powers left then, rather swiftly, and Ryan came back with a wry grin. 'Oops,' he murmured.

'I'm sorry,' Ginny began, but he waved her apology aside.

'No. Don't be,' he said softly. 'It isn't your fault—it had to happen sooner or later.'

'But it's the first time I've been here, and they're going to think we've been carrying on under the children's noses.'

'No. I told them we haven't. I told them nothing will happen while the children are in the house with us—I also told them I'm not a monk and they're going to have to respect that. They have to realise that I'm still alive and I need to move on. That doesn't mean I didn't love their daughter and don't regret her death. Of course I do, but I wasn't buried with her and I don't see why I should behave as though I was. Anyway, this is nothing to do with Ann. This is quite separate.'

Category Three, she thought, whatever he might say to the contrary. Oh, well. He perched on the arm of the garden bench beside her and looked down at her. 'Can I get you a drink?'

She pushed the pain inside out of the way and smiled up at him. 'How about a stiff gin?' she said drily.

He chuckled. 'Not too stiff—you're driving later. G and T?'

'Lovely.'

He came back with two tall glasses clinking with ice,

the condensation streaming down the outside, and sat beside her this time—his long legs in khaki shorts stretched
out beside her.

'How come your legs aren't blue?' she said indignantly.

'What?'

She hitched up her skirt to mid-thigh and he chuckled.
'Whoops. New jeans?'

'Unfortunately, yes. I wanted the deep-dye ones because
they don't get so grubby. Perhaps I should have gone for
stonewashed.'

'What do you call being tumbled around on the river
bed if it isn't stonewashed?' he teased.

'Provocation—and the next time you want to draw attention to my bust could you do so out of range of the
children, for safety?'

He chuckled, and the chuckle turned into a laugh, and
then they were both laughing helplessly. When they
stopped rolling around on their seats and opened their eyes
the children were lined up in front of them, looking puzzled.

'Why are you laughing?' Evie asked, her head cocked
to one side in unconscious imitation of Ryan.

'Nothing, sweetheart,' Ryan wheezed, and wiped his
eyes. 'Nothing at all. Just a bit of a wet joke.'

That set him off again, but the children were still there,
and Gus looked crotchety and fed up. She smiled at them.
'Don't pay any attention to your father,' she said. 'It's just
his sense of humour.'

Gus tugged at his sleeve. 'Daddy?'

He pulled himself together and grinned at his son. 'Wat-
cha, kid. What's the matter?'

'Are you going to cook now? I'm starving,' Gus said
plaintively.

'Of course—sorry, son. I'll light the barbeque now.'

It was a gas one, and within minutes he had chicken tikka kebabs and sizzling bacon and pineapple rolls and all sorts of other little titbits all under way. He gave Ginny the job of shredding the salad, but when she brought it out there was a moment of tension.

'Daddy doesn't make the salad like that,' Gus said, eyeing it suspiciously. 'He cuts it all up small.'

'Like Mummy did.'

There was a tense silence, then Ryan cleared his throat and took the bowl from her. 'It's nice to have a change. More exciting. I was beginning to get fed up with having it the same old way and, you know, lots of people do it like this. Actually, we used to cut it up small because you were just babies, but grown-ups usually have their salad like this, in fact. Try it.'

He set it down on the patio table and the children eyed it—and him—with suspicion. Then Evie reached for the salad servers. 'I think it looks nicer like this,' she said. 'I expect Gus will still need his cut up small, though.'

'I do not! I can manage it too!' her small brother protested, and Ginny hid her smile.

How cleverly he had got them out of that awkward situation, she realised. How many others would there be? Maybe none. Maybe after the fiasco with Ann's parents he wouldn't let her near his family again.

And that would be for the best, she thought, because those delightful little people, so like their father in so many ways, were in danger of stealing what little was left of her heart...

On Monday she was back to work, and true to form it was as hectic as ever. People who had been too busy over the weekend to come to see them all poured in off the streets with a variety of maladies, most of which they could easily have treated themselves at home. Others were well within the scope of the average GP and only a few really needed a doctor's attention. Most of those were people who should, in fact, have come in sooner.

One woman presented with a swollen right foot and a classic horseshoe bruise around the back of her heel, and said that as she'd been driving on Friday morning to a conference she'd had a terrible pain in the top of her foot. She'd been unable to stop because she'd been on the M25, and so had carried on.

'What were you doing?' Ginny asked her, looking at the foot in puzzlement. The bruise indicated a fracture, but how could she have fractured it doing nothing?

'I had my foot bent up at the pedals—that's all.'

'What were you wearing?'

'High-heeled ankle boots—laced ones with little hooks at the top.'

'Tight?'

'Not really—well, yes, I suppose so when my foot's bent.'

Ginny pursed her lips. 'I wonder—do you do a lot of walking?'

The woman laughed. 'Not for pleasure. I don't have time. But, yes, I suppose I do. I'm on my feet all day, anyway.'

'Any pain the previous day?'

She laughed again. 'No more than usual—although, now you come to mention it, I have had an ache over that part of my foot for the past week or so but I've been too busy to pay it any attention.'

Ginny nodded. 'Right, I think we need it X-rayed because, although it seems unlikely, you might have got a fracture of one of the long, thin bones in your foot.'

'A fracture? How?'

'Stress—repetitive action, in your case, probably walking. Either that or you popped a ligament while you were driving. Let's take some pictures and check, then we'll go from there.'

It was, indeed, a fracture. She showed the woman where it was on the X-ray. 'Oh, yes,' she said, 'that's exactly where it hurts! Well, how odd.'

'It's called a March fracture. It's a classic military fracture sustained by infantrymen as a result of walking long distances. Unfortunately for you, you don't have to be in the military to get one!'

'So, what do I have to do?'

'Rest it, ice-pack it, wear a support bandage and elevate it. Just remember RICE—rest, ice, compression and elevation. It should heal after a couple of weeks or so, but only if you give it a chance.'

'But I can't do all that! I've got work to do—I've got to be in three meetings today, another one tomorrow in Manchester, on Friday I've got a site meeting with a designer—I can't afford to miss any of them.'

'In which case, we'd better put a cast on it and give you some crutches and just hope for the best, but you'll have to rest with it up as much as possible to stop it swelling inside the cast. In fact, I think we'll put a sort of open cast on it just in case it does swell in this heat, but you really must pay attention to it. If it hurts you're doing too much. What do you do, exactly?'

'I'm an architect.'

'How interesting,' Ginny said as she filled in the notes. 'What sort of buildings?'

'Houses—domestic architecture generally. I work for one of the big construction companies. We do upmarket, unusual properties. I'm very lucky to have the job. I could

be designing starter homes and three-bedroomed semis—
or I could be unemployed. I really can't afford to foul up.'

'Well, take it as easy as you can, come back and see us
in a week for a check-up, and if you know you're doing
too much you'll have to stop. I'll give you a letter, and I
want you to promise you'll be sensible.'

'I can't,' she said honestly.

Ginny laughed and shook her head. 'At least you don't
lie about it! Well, do your best.'

She sent her off with a letter for her employers and a
request for a cast and some crutches, and was just about
to call the next patient when an ambulance came in with
a man with severe abdominal pain.

'Bring him straight in to me,' she told the triage nurse.

He was in his mid fifties, obviously in excruciating pain
and almost speechless.

'Where does it hurt?' she asked him. 'Can you show
me?'

He pointed to the centre of his abdomen. 'It goes into
my back,' he groaned, and then retched helplessly.

'OK, let's have a look,' she said, peeling back the blanket. His abdomen wasn't rigid, which ruled out perforation
in any form, and made aortic aneurysm or heart attack
more likely. She listened to his heart, but apart from beating fast it sounded normal.

Gently palpating his abdomen, she found a soft, tender
mass in the midline. 'What's his blood pressure?' she
asked the nurse.

'Low—ninety over forty.'

'Get a surgical registrar down here, could you, fast? I
think it's a leaking aneurysm. Mr Bright, I'm going to put
a needle into one of your veins and give you some fluids
and some painkillers. You'd better have some oxygen, too,
to help you breathe more easily.'

She put the mask on, found a vein and set up the large-bore IV line in record time, and after taking blood for cross-matching and analysis she started running in plasma expander to boost his blood volume. His blood pressure was dropping slowly, and she didn't want to allow it to become too low, in case of a sudden deterioration of the aorta.

The radiographer came and took some X-rays with the portable machine, and then Ross Hamilton arrived and confirmed her diagnosis.

'Tom Russell's in Theatre now—I'll get him to do Mr Bright straight away. Has he vomited?'

'Yes—his stomach's completely empty.'

'Good. Right, let's get him up there and prepped and he can go straight in. I'll ring Theatre.'

The staff nurse popped her head round the curtain. 'Got an RTA coming in on a blue light—Ryan wants you in Resus as soon as you're available.'

'OK. Tell him I'll be with him shortly,' she said. She filled in Mr Bright's notes, speeded up the drip and sent him off with a nurse and a porter to Theatre.

Then she went down to Resus, just as the ambulance arrived. The team went to the door to meet it, and as the trolley was unloaded the paramedic was firing information at them.

'Casualty unconscious at the scene, no obvious head injury, abdominal and chest injuries from seat belt on impact, leg injuries from the bulkhead—two small children in the car with her unhurt. They're with the police pending identification. Low blood pressure, so we've got a line in and we're giving her saline—took some bloods for cross-match, here—'

He handed over a bundle of tubes and Ginny took them and followed the trolley down the corridor. He was still talking but Ginny could only catch the odd word. It was academic. The woman needed immediate and comprehensive assistance—that much was obvious—and Ryan would programme the team.

She dealt with the blood, sending it off immediately for cross-matching, and turned back to where Ryan was working on the patient.

The patient had a back and neck brace on and, because of the possibility of neck injury Ryan inserted a breathing tube by pulling her chin forwards without extending her neck.

ABCDE, she thought. Airway was dealt with. Next was breathing, and she put an oxygen mask over the woman's face and started to administer one hundred per cent oxygen.

Circulation was the next item, and her blood pressure was low. 'Get a surgeon in here, please, we might have a haemorrhage,' Ryan said, his head bent over the patient.

'Ross is about—he might still be on the unit,' Ginny told him.

Just then the door opened and Ross stuck his head round it. 'Do you need me, by any chance, as I'm down here?'

'Oh, good man. Yes, we've got a woman with query abdominal haemorrhage—she's unconscious and her blood pressure's crashing. Chest and leg injuries as well—take a look, could you?'

They stepped back to give Ross access to the patient, and Ginny watched in horror as the blood drained from his face.

'Dear God, no,' he whispered in anguish. 'Lizzi?'

Ryan swore softly and turned to him, but he was too slow. Ross drew a steadying breath, stepped forward and put his hands on her abdomen. They were shaking, but he was feeling, carefully exploring, looking for answers.

'She's got a few broken ribs but her chest wall's moving all right,' Ginny said to Ryan.

'Get an anaesthetist down here,' he snapped over her head. 'We may have to open her up to find this leak. Any sign of a pneumothorax?'

She shook her head. 'Not so far.' She shot Ross a look, and turned back to Ryan. 'Who is she?' she mouthed.

'His wife.'

Ginny's mouth made a silent O, and she looked down at the naked woman lying on the table. Her chest was crushed and bruised, her face and temple now swelling, her legs deformed below the knee.

And, whatever he had found, Ross wasn't happy.

'I can feel something low down,' he said. 'I don't think it's her spleen. I'll have to operate—'

'No way,' Ryan said firmly. 'Is Oliver in the building?'

'He's on his way.'

The door was shouldered briskly open then, and a man in surgical pyjamas took Ross firmly by the shoulders and almost lifted him out of the way.

'Lower left quadrant,' Ross said hoarsely, standing back to watch him.

'Yes,' Oliver agreed. 'I think it's gynaecological, actually. She's got a heavy vaginal bleed started; she may be aborting or it could be a ruptured ectopic pregnancy—is that possible? I don't think she's had an abdominal injury, there's no sign of any impact. What happened?'

'Don't know,' Ryan said. 'There were no other cars involved.'

'She is pregnant,' Ross said numbly. Then, as the situation began to sink in, he seized Ryan's arm. 'What about the kids? Where are they? Where are the babies?'

Ginny took his arm and led him out. 'They're all right.

They're with the police. They weren't hurt. Come on, let's go and find out where they are now.'

'But Lizzi—'

'—is in good hands. The best. Don't worry, she'll be all right.'

'She's unconscious,' he said, as if he'd just registered it.

Behind them, through the swinging door, they heard Ryan's voice. 'Damn. She's arrested.'

Ross froze, then seemed to crumple before her eyes. 'Dear God, no, not my Lizzi…' He shook with silent sobs, but there were no tears. He was deeply shocked, she realised, and she led him to the interview room and sat him down where he had had to give so many people bad news, and held his hands and talked to him while he coped with the wave of fear which was threatening to swamp him…

Then the door opened and a nurse came in. 'Ryan wants you back there, please,' she said to Ginny.

Ross leapt to his feet. 'How is she? She arrested—is she dead?' he asked, grabbing her arm.

The nurse looked surprised that he knew. 'No, she's alive. Her heart's going again. Do you want some tea?'

He shook his head. 'No, I want to be in there.'

'I don't think—'

Ginny left them arguing about it and went back to Resus. Ryan lifted his head and looked at her across Lizzi Hamilton's battered body. 'How is he?'

'Shocked. How's she?'

'Grim. She arrested.'

'We know. We heard you.'

'Damn. I didn't want him worried any more than he had to be. Where is he?'

'Interview room with a nurse.'

'Good. I hope she keeps him there. We're going to open her up and clamp whatever it is that's bleeding in there.'

'Down here? Not in Theatre?'

'No time,' he told her. 'We've got a gynae team coming down but I need help up here with this chest. She's got a tension pneumothorax now. Can you help me put a drain in?'

She did as she was told—working almost mechanically—thinking all the time of Ross out there in the interview room.

Except that he wasn't. He came in, despite protests from the team, leant against the wall and watched them in grim-lipped silence as they struggled for Lizzi's life.

She arrested again, and they got her going again, and then the gynae team arrived as the anaesthetist knocked her out and they opened her up and discovered a ruptured ectopic pregnancy with a torn vein pouring blood into her abdomen.

It was clamped, sucked out, more blood squeezed into her veins by the nursing team and within moments she showed a better colour and her blood pressure picked up.

'That's more like it,' Ryan said softly. 'Come on, Lizzi, you can do it.'

They removed the ruptured Fallopian tube, cleaned up the mess, closed the incision and then the anaesthetist reversed the anaesthetic. 'Let's see if she's still unconscious,' Ryan murmured. 'Lizzi? Lizzi, wake up, can you hear me?'

'I'll talk to her,' Ross said, elbowing Ryan out of the way. 'Lizzi-love? Wake up, come on. Time to get up. Lizzi?' He squeezed her hand. 'Lizzi? Wake up, darling, come on, now.'

'No,' she moaned through bruised lips. 'Hurt.'

Ross's eyes fluttered closed, then he bent over and

kissed her forehead, emotions chasing across his taut features. 'I know, sweetheart. You're all right now, though. I'm here.'

'Children—'

'They're fine. Don't worry.'

'Where am I?'

'At the hospital. Open your eyes, darling.'

'Pupils equal and reactive,' Ryan confirmed. 'We've got her back.'

His voice was quiet but a little flat—strained, in a way. Ginny looked at him for the first time in several minutes, and was shocked at the change in him. His face was grey, his eyes hollow and somehow dull, and without another word he turned and walked out of the room.

She couldn't follow him—she was still too busy with their patient—but he was back a moment later, his colour a little better.

His eyes were just as blank, though, and he worked almost mechanically.

'Right, now the excitement's over can we have some X-rays of her legs, chest, spine, head, pelvis and anything else that hurts? Then she'd better go up to Orthopaedics for those legs.'

'She's in a lot of pain,' Ross told him from his position at her head.

'We'll get that under control. Right, Ginny, thank you for your help. If you want to go and get on?'

She nodded, and squeezed Ross's arm. 'I'm glad she's all right.'

He smiled weakly. 'Thanks.'

She left them to it, with one last glance at Ryan's taut face. Why was he looking so grim? Perhaps it was just all a little too close to home.

*   *   *

Ryan thought he was going to pass out. His stomach was rebelling, his head was reeling and he could hardly think for the roaring in his ears. He had to get Lizzi admitted, though, and then he could get out of here.

Did it always take so long? It seemed for ever before she was transferred, Ross in tow, and the police programmed to bring the children in to him as soon as possible.

Ryan tugged off his gloves, threw them in the bin, stripped off his bloody white coat and headed for the door, ignoring the looks of his staff. He just had to get out before the walls caved in on him and he threw up.

It was cooler than it had been at the weekend, and he went through the doors and sucked in great lungfuls of air. His car was parked near the door in the slot reserved for the consultants, and he opened it and sat sideways in the driver's seat, his head in his hands—waiting for the dizziness to recede.

It was Ross's face that had done it. It could have been himself, looking in a mirror. The shock, the fear, the clinical calm while you assess what needs to be assessed—except that Ross's wife had been alive, and his had been dead.

There had been no doubt. Ann's head had cracked like an egg and the side of her skull was crushed in. Nobody lived through injuries like that. Still, he'd checked her pulse, or tried to. Her wrist had been smashed and his fingers had come away with splinters of bone.

Bile rose in his throat and he leant back, swallowing hard. It was talking to Virginia on Saturday that had brought it all back. He'd shut it out for years, but that conversation had opened the door to it and now, fighting to save Lizzi, it all came flooding back in glorious Technicolor.

A shadow fell over him. 'O'Connor?'

He opened his eyes and saw Virginia there, silhouetted against the sky—the sun behind her turning her hair to a halo. Was she a saint? She'd have to be—to understand this.

'Are you all right?'

He nodded. 'Just a bit queasy. I'll be fine.'

'Bit close to home?' she murmured.

He nodded again. 'You just remember all the things you thought you'd forgotten. It all gets a bit personal.'

'Why don't you go home for the rest of the day? Jack's here. We can manage without you.'

How tempting. 'I may do that. Are you sure you can cope?'

'Oh, we'll struggle on,' she said with a smile. 'Are you OK to drive?'

He considered that. 'I will be. I'll just sit here for a bit.'

'Go to my flat and lie down if you like.'

His eyes searched hers. 'Could I? Do you mind?'

Her hand cupped his cheek, soft and gentle, her touch somehow cleansing. 'Of course I don't mind. Here, take the key.'

She handed him a bunch of keys and he caught her hand in his and kissed it. 'Thanks,' he whispered. He couldn't speak any louder; there was a huge lump in his throat and if she didn't go away and stop being nice to him he was going to make a fool of himself.

He was safe. She went without any further delay and after a few more minutes he drove round to her flat, stripped off his clothes and crawled into the bed. Sleep claimed him in seconds, bringing blessed oblivion and much-needed rest for his troubled mind.

He woke much later to the sound of her moving around

in the living-room and, throwing back the bedclothes, he stood up and went over to the doorway.

She didn't hear him at first, and carried on tidying newspapers and patting cushions. She had changed into a soft, floaty dress of Indian cotton that swirled shapelessly round her slender form, and he was suddenly wide awake and consumed by a ravenous hunger.

'Virginia,' he said, and his voice sounded sleep-rough and gravelly. She turned and looked at him with a slow, womanly smile, and without a word she went into his arms and kissed him.

The dress was easily disposed of, and the little scrappy lace briefs, and then he was buried in her body, cradled in the soft heat of her womanhood, sheltered from the horror of the past few hours. Her arms held him close, her legs circled him, and with a rough cry he gave himself up to the need that threatened to overwhelm him.

Ginny held him, swept along by the demon that drove him and stunned by the wild, wordless passion that fought its way out of him. His mouth was on hers, hard and demanding; his hands were rough on her breasts, and yet not too rough, never hurting her—just wakening some wild part of her she hadn't known existed.

He was insatiable, his body's power directed to their pleasure and yet somehow neither of them could reach that elusive peak. They clamoured at each other, nails raking, mouths biting, bodies arching, until suddenly without warning Ginny felt a huge explosion of sensation rip out from the centre of her body and nearly tear her apart.

Dimly she felt Ryan stiffen and cry out, then she was falling, falling, slowly coming back down to earth and to the awareness of his heart pounding against hers, the sweat-slicked feel of his skin against her palms, the weight of his body collapsed against her chest.

He was silent for an age, then he lifted his head and looked down at her, his eyes concerned.

'I'm sorry,' he said hoarsely. 'That got a little wild. Are you OK?'

She nodded. 'Are you?'

'I think so. I guess we're both alive.'

'I would say so.'

He dropped his head back against her shoulder. 'Sometimes this job gets a little too much,' he murmured. 'I'm sorry if I hurt you.'

'You didn't.' She stroked the damp skin of his back, and he rolled to his side and looked into her eyes.

'You're being very understanding. Most women would have told me to go to hell until I'd got my head together.'

'Most women haven't got any imagination, then.'

His smile was wan. 'How's Lizzi?'

'OK. They've reduced her leg fractures under a light anaesthetic to restore her circulation. She's got to have an operation tomorrow to plate one but they wanted to let her stabilise and get a bit stronger.'

'Head injury?'

'No. Just mild concussion. The ectopic was the thing that caused it, apparently. She suddenly had this terrible pain and lost control of the car.'

'Did the children and Ross get reunited?'

'Yes. They were fine. He's taken them home.'

His hand came up and cupped her cheek, his touch tender now and infinitely caring. 'Virginia?'

She searched his eyes. 'Yes?' she whispered.

'This is nothing to do with Ann. The shock was, this afternoon, but now, with us—this is just because we're still alive; because every now and again you come face-to-face with death and you need to be sure you're still in there somewhere, still human, and the beast hasn't got you yet.'

His hand smoothed her hair back and he kissed her forehead lovingly. 'Thanks for being here for me.'

She couldn't speak. Too many emotions crowded her mind; too many tears blocked her throat. She just hugged him, and he held her for a moment before releasing her.

'I need to fetch my kids from Betty. They went back to school today, and she takes them home afterwards and I collect them from her when I get away from work. I usually ring her if I'm going to be late.'

'Use the phone,' she said.

'Mmm.' He swung his legs over the side of the bed and rummaged for his clothes then dragged them on, before going into the living-room and picking up the phone. Ginny lay there, listening to him as he told Ann's mother he'd been held up at work.

'A colleague's wife was involved in a serious accident. It's taken rather a long time to sort things out,' he said. 'I'll be over shortly.'

He put the phone down and came back into the bedroom. 'She said not to hurry; she's going to feed them.' The bed dipped under his weight. 'Fancy fish and chips?'

'There's a chippy round the corner.'

'I know.'

She smiled. 'All right. You go and get them; I'll get up and put the kettle on.'

He went out and she boiled the kettle, made a pot of tea and finished the tidying up she'd been doing when he distracted her.

She paused, a cushion in her hand, and thought of what he'd said about the beast. Yes, she thought, sudden and violent death was a beast that stalked them all, especially those who worked amongst its havoc. Face-to-face with it, as they so often were, it was no wonder that their reaction was often wild and untamed.

It needed to be—to match the beast for strength, and win…

CHAPTER SIX

THE sole topic of conversation in the department the next day was Lizzi Hamilton's accident. Ginny arrived in the morning to the steady hum of the grapevine, and was immediately included.

Ross was there, propping up the wall with his rangy frame, looking tired but ten years younger than he had the day before. He greeted Ginny with a weary smile.

'Hi,' she said cheerfully, relieved to see his obviously much happier frame of mind. 'How are things?'

'Oh, she's OK. She's had a bit of a rough night—her chest hurts because of her ribs and because Ryan thumped her so hard to get her going again, and her incision and legs are giving her hell, but her head injury hasn't turned into anything nasty. She's upset about the baby, of course, but that was obviously the cause of the accident. She remembers this awful pain, and then losing control of the car. Nothing much after that, which is perhaps just as well. She was lucky to get away with it so lightly, really.'

They were all thoughtful for a moment, remembering the scene and how close the beast had come.

'How does she look?' Ginny asked, remembering also her bruised face and temple.

Ross laughed without humour. 'Colourful. She's got one hell of a black eye—still, it matches the rest of her body.'

'And how are the children?'

He sighed. 'Oh, OK, I suppose. Her mother's got them now. I brought them in early to see her because they were fretting and so was she, but the little one's too small to understand and the older one was upset by the tubes and the bruises, so it wasn't overwhelmingly successful as far as they were concerned. Lizzi was pleased to see that they were all right, though, so I suppose it served its purpose.'

He shrugged himself away from the wall. 'Anyway, thanks to all of you for all you did yesterday. You were marvellous.'

'All part of the service,' Jack said with a grin. 'Anyway, it's Ryan you really want to thank and he's not in today. His kids are sick.'

Ginny felt all the colour go out of her day. She had wondered where he was. Knowing that he wasn't going to be in today took the edge off it somewhat.

She rang him later at home, and caught him sounding harassed.

'They're both vomiting, and so are Betty and Doug. It must have been something they ate. I'm trying to get a babysitter so I can get in, but they don't want me to leave them.'

'So don't,' she said practically. 'Jack's here, so is Patrick Haddon, I'm in—there are plenty of staff around. Just stay there and look after them and put your feet up.'

He snorted. 'That'd be a fine thing. I've spent the morning changing sheets and mopping up.'

'Need a hand later?' she offered.

Talk about a drowning man clutching at straws. 'What time can you get here?' he asked.

'About five-thirty? I can't stay late, though, because I'm on duty tomorrow night, so I'll need to get to bed early tonight.'

'Whatever. You couldn't bring me something to eat, could you? The kitchen's empty and I can't leave them to get to the shops. I've got half a loaf of bread, some mouldy cheese and a limp lettuce.'

'Ploughmans lunch?' she suggested.

He made a rude noise, and she chuckled. 'And you,' she said. 'I'll see you later. I'll do what I can.'

She had cause to regret her optimism later. Although there were several medical staff there, they ran into a busy spell and they were all rushed off their feet.

'Don't suppose there's any chance of Ryan coming in?' Jack said to her in passing.

'Don't think so,' she told him. 'Not unless I go and relieve him, and I've only met the children once.'

'Forget it. We don't need to lose you too. We'll cope.'

They did, but only by the skin of their teeth, and just as they were getting ready to go home the evening rush started.

'Want me to hang on for a bit?' she offered.

'Would you?' Jack said gratefully. 'I'd like to get this lot cleared before we abandon ship for the night.'

So she rang Ryan and told him she'd be a little late, and then wondered why she hadn't made her escape while the going was good. There were two road accidents—one unfortunately fatal and one with multiple injuries, although not as dramatic as Lizzi Hamilton's—and then, just when that lot was sorted out, a child decided to play Superman and leapt out of the bedroom window.

It wouldn't have been so bad if his bedroom hadn't been right over the greenhouse.

He came in on a blue light, sirens screaming, and they had O negative blood standing by to transfuse him immediately. The ambulance man had taken some blood for cross-matching, and so they were able to start the transfusion as soon as they could get a line in.

And that, as she discovered, wasn't easy. He wouldn't keep still, his arms and legs were cut to shreds and the only vein she could find was in his neck.

'I think I'll need some help with this one,' she told the mother, and called for Jack.

'Oh, my,' he said softly, and with a minimum of fuss got the line in. The boy was getting quieter anyway, with the loss of blood, and she set up the IV drip and started to run in the first unit of blood, then turned back to the lacerations to continue her search for the worst leaks.

He had just missed the radial artery in his left wrist, which was just as well or he would have died in minutes, but Jack wasn't happy to treat him on the unit.

'He needs to go to Theatre and have that lot stitched under a general anaesthetic. We can't give him that much lignocaine, and anyway it'll take hours. I'll just catch the worst ones together to stop the blood gushing out, and we'll get a surgeon on the job. We need X-rays first, though, for any fragments of glass left in him.'

And after he was despatched, complete with glass in his bottom for removal by the surgeons, she was able to go home, wash and change and go to Ryan's house via the supermarket.

He greeted her with rapture. 'I am so hungry I could eat roots,' he said, snatching the bag and heading for the kitchen.

'Good job I got potatoes and carrots, then, isn't it?' she teased and, going up on her toes, she kissed his cheek. 'How are the little darlings?'

He sighed and raked his hand through his hair. 'Vile. Evie's better now and demanding attention, of course, but Angus is still very volatile. He ate more of everything than Evie, being a pig, and of course he's smaller. They had a take-away, apparently.'

'Daddy?'

He went to the bottom of the stairs, resignation written on his face. 'Yes, Evie, what is it, sweetheart?'

'Who's that?'

'Virginia.'

Silence for a second, then, 'I want a story.'

He sighed and rested his head against the banisters. 'Again?' he murmured.

'Can I read to her?'

He looked at Ginny as if she'd just sprouted wings. 'Could you? *Black Beauty*—it's on her bedside table. It's always on her bedside table. I'll bring you up a cup of tea.'

He did—and they both ignored it and carried on with the story, because it was the bit where Ginger died and Ginny was as riveted as Ryan's little daughter. Finally, though, Evie flagged and snuggled down against Ginny, and she put the book down and sang a nursery rhyme she remembered from her childhood. And then, after Evie was asleep, she sat there, still humming softly and wondering how she would have felt if life hadn't played her such an impoverished hand.

The little body resting against hers was so vulnerable. So dependent. Nobody and nothing depended on Ginny to that extent. Ryan was Evie's world, the hub of her universe. Ginny wondered what it was like to be the hub of someone else's universe.

A tie, to be sure, but what a sweet tie.

She looked down at the little blonde head and stroked the hair gently back from her sleep-flushed face. Such a pretty child. How sad that she had lost her mother when she was so young. Who would tell her all the things mothers told their teenage daughters?

Betty? Ginny shrank from the thought. She seemed so repressed, so correct. How would she deal with a teenager's raging hormones in this difficult day and age?

She could hear Ryan moving around in the room next

door, dealing with Gus in the grip of another crisis. He needed a wife, she thought, although he wasn't ready yet for that.

Still, there was always Category Three.

At least that would keep his spirits up and his morale intact while he fought the good fight.

He appeared in the doorway, looking drained. 'I think he might settle now. I've just changed his sheets and given him a wash, and he's kept some electrolyte replacement down.'

'Vile stuff,' she said softly. 'If he can keep that down he is better.'

They shared a smile, albeit a weary one, and he held out his hand. 'Come and have a drink—did you have supper?'

She shook her head. 'No. I didn't get round to it. Sorry I was so late, it all went supernova after I phoned you.'

'Always the way.' He slung his arm round her shoulder as they went downstairs, and at the bottom he drew her into his arms. 'I've missed you today,' he murmured into her hair. 'It's been hell here. They were going like geysers first thing this morning—they started about four o'clock, and I thought Angus was never going to stop.'

'How are your in-laws?'

'The outlaws, you mean?' he said with a grin, letting her go and walking into the kitchen. 'Oh, they're improving. I'm going to take the kids round to them tomorrow and they can all be weak and feeble together. They'll spend the night there tomorrow, anyway, because I'm on duty overnight with you.'

It was hospital policy never to have a junior member of the medical staff on call unsupported by a senior member of the team, and so the senior staff took it in turns to sleep in the hospital. Usually they were undisturbed, but there had been occasions when Ginny, at least, had been glad to have the backup available.

Knowing it was there was somehow reassuring.

She leant against the worktop and folded her arms. 'My moral support,' she said with a smile.

'You are allowed to wake me,' he reminded her teasingly. 'My sleep isn't sacrosanct.'

'Ah, but if I come in your room I might not get out again for ages, and the patient could be better off with me on my own than with neither of us while I spend ages waking you!'

He pulled her into his arms and nuzzled her neck. 'I could just take you to bed now,' he mumbled. 'You smell wonderful.'

'You don't,' she told him bluntly. 'You have a distinct aroma of the sick-room, but I guess I'll put up with it.'

He released her instantly. 'Give me five minutes,' he said, and was gone. It took him ten but, to be fair, he had showered, washed his hair and dressed in fresh clothes.

'Better?' he said with a boyish grin.

Lord, she loved that grin and the sparkle in those glorious green eyes. 'Much,' she confirmed. 'You can have a hug now.'

'How about some supper?'

She grinned. 'It's probably better for me, but the hug's awfully tempting.'

He chuckled. 'Eat first, hug later.'

'I have to go later.'

'So you do. Probably just as well. I promised Betty and Doug no hanky-panky in the house with the kids. I tell you what, we'll sit on the sofa and watch the television and eat off our knees—OK? Then I can hug you at the same time.'

So they did, and they fed each other titbits and watched

the news and laughed softly, and then Ryan went out to the kitchen to make some coffee and Ginny looked around the room, noticing it for the first time.

And in the corner, on the piano, there was a photo of a blonde woman with shining hair and laughing eyes, and Ryan's arm was round her, and the children were in front of her, and Ginny felt the bottom drop out of her world.

It was all very well to sit down with him after helping to put the children to bed, and eat a meal he had prepared from food she had bought, and generally play house—but that was all she was doing.

Playing house.

She didn't belong here, she never would. He didn't want her in his life in that way and, although she'd always known happy ever after wouldn't come her way, somehow it still hurt.

Category Three, she reminded herself. Sex slave. Not wife, and certainly not mother.

Never mother.

She stood up, tears clogging her throat, and bumped into Ryan who was just coming back into the room with two steaming mugs of coffee.

'I have to go. I'm tired. Do you mind if I don't stay for coffee?'

'But it's made,' he protested. 'Stay and drink it—it won't take five minutes.'

'You have mine,' she said with a forced smile. 'I have to go. Night, O'Connor, Sleep tight.'

She didn't wait for a kiss, even. Ryan, puzzled, went into the sitting-room and put the cups down, then looked around. Whatever had got into her?

His eyes lit on the photo of him and the children with Ann, and suddenly he knew what it was.

'Damn,' he whispered softly and, picking up the photo,

he polished the glass with his sleeve, then looked down at the image of his laughing wife. 'Oh, Ann,' he said heavily, 'what am I going to do about her?'

Ginny drove home, dry-eyed but with an aching hollow inside. She didn't belong there with Ryan and his family, and she was crazy to let herself play little games.

It was dangerous—altogether too foolish for words. It was one thing to indulge herself with an affair, quite another to involve his children and to make herself important to them. It probably hadn't even occurred to Ryan that the children might get dependent on her, but it had occurred to her—and, also that she might get too dependent on them.

She was already in danger of that, she realised. As she'd sat tonight, reading aloud to that tired, pale little girl, she had wanted nothing more than to wrap her arms round the tiny frame and keep her safe while she slept.

So foolish. So very, very foolish.

She went into her flat, flicking on lights and heading for the kitchen, and there on the window-sill—waiting for her—was Geronimo.

She let him in. 'You're late, sweetheart. Come and have a cuddle,' she murmured, and picked him up. She could allow herself to love the cat. That was safe.

Geronimo, though, had other ideas. Instead of snuggling down against her shoulder as usual, he was fussy and she put him on the floor. He went straight to the fridge and sat down in front of it, watching her over his shoulder as if he couldn't believe how slow she could be.

'Hungry, eh? You've got a home.'

He miaowed at her.

'Oh, all right. Here, there's some tuna left. Want that?'

He did, and a little piece of cheese, and a saucer of milk.

Then she put him out again and watched as he ran down the garden and nipped over the wall.

Five minutes later he was back again, winding round her legs and looking restless.

How odd, she thought. He always goes home at night, and she always lets him in.

Ginny went down the garden and tried to peer over the wall, but she was too short. She looked around, and spied the bench. It was heavy, but she managed to drag it across to the end wall and climbed up on the back.

The house was in darkness, but for the flickering light of a television in the back room downstairs. It seemed odd that she didn't have any lights on. There was usually one upstairs by this time, if not more than one.

The cat went into the garden again and cried at the door, but there was no sign of life. Perhaps she'd gone away, or been taken into hospital.

Leaving the television on?

Ginny sighed. She couldn't just ignore it. Fetching a torch from inside, she went back down the garden, shinned over the wall and dropped down into Geronimo's garden.

She smashed a cold frame on the way, the tinkling of glass bringing lights on in the next-door house but nothing in Geronimo's.

She felt silly now, creeping around in someone's garden in the middle of the night. The old lady had probably dozed off in front of the television and forgotten to put a light on, that was all. How was Ginny going to explain her presence when she was caught? She'd probably give the old dear the fright of her life!

She tapped on the door first and called, but there was nothing. She did it again, louder this time, and then she thought she heard a feeble cry.

Her brows twitching together, she went over to the back

room window and shone the torch inside. She couldn't see anything, though. 'Hello?' she called. 'Are you all right? I'm a doctor.'

Anyone could say that, she thought, and felt a little foolish. She heard movement in the house next door and an upstairs window was flung open.

'Hey, you! What's going on?'

She shone the torch at herself so that the woman could see her. 'I live over the wall at the bottom—I wondered if she was all right. Have you heard anything?'

'No—hang on, I'll come down and let you in. I've got a key.'

She waited, and after a moment the hall light came on, then the back room, then the kitchen. There was a scrape as the key was turned, then the woman opened the door and let her in.

'Have you found her?'

'No—let's look in here—oh, good gracious, Mabel, what have you done, dear?'

A very frail elderly lady was sitting on the loo—a ghastly pallor on her face—leaning against the wall and clutching at the grab-handle beside her with one gnarled and misshapen hand. The other hand lay useless in her lap, and one side of her face was slumped in a classic post-stroke paralysis.

Ginny had no idea how long she'd been there, but her relief when she realised she'd been rescued was obvious and she began to weep soundlessly.

She didn't speak, though, and Ginny realised that her stroke had affected her speech centre and so she had been unable to cry for help or answer, although she must have heard all the kerfuffle. Hence the feeble, wordless cry she had heard when she knocked.

'I'll call an ambulance—you stay with her. Did I hear you say you're a doctor?' Dora said.

'Yes, that's right,' she said absently. 'Mabel, don't worry now, all right? We'll soon have you more comfortable. Dora's gone to call an ambulance, and we'll get you into a nice comfy bed and make sure you're all right. OK?'

She nodded tearfully, and Ginny knelt down on the tiled floor of the cold little bathroom and held Mabel's hands and told her that she had fed Geronimo, and Mabel wasn't to worry about him—he could live with her in the flat for now.

'I hear you calling him every night, but tonight he was still around. That's why I came to see if anything had happened, because of him—so you ought to be grateful to him, really, even if he is a thief and stole my bacon.'

Well, that was a good sign. If you knew what you were looking for it was almost a smile!

The ambulance came a short while later, and Mabel was borne off to hospital, leaving Ginny to climb back over the fence because she had no other way of getting into her flat. The ambulance man gave her a leg-up before he left, and she watched Mabel's exit from the top of the wall before letting herself down, scooping up the restless cat and going into the flat.

He spent the night on her bed, quite happily, and in the morning she put him out, fed him outside and went to work. She didn't have time to run backwards and forwards today, and even if she had she wouldn't have done so. If she had any spare time she intended to spend it getting to know her neighbour.

Conversation would be tricky, she was sure, but probably not as tricky as her conversation with Ryan could be.

Her conversation with Ryan turned out to be so tricky that she never had it. Why was it, she thought later, that when you had something difficult and important to say the moment never seemed to present itself, and so you were left endlessly in suspense?

The day was just too darned hectic, and she shot back during the early evening to wash and change, grab a bite to eat and feed the cat again.

Another tin of tuna bit the dust because she hadn't had time to get to the shops for cat food, but he didn't seem to mind.

She was just about to leave for the hospital again when her bleeper squawked. She rang the switchboard and was connected to Ryan.

'Where are you?' he asked.

'Home. I had to feed the cat; my neighbour had a stroke yesterday and I ended up rescuing her last night. What's the problem?'

'No problem. I wanted to talk to you, that's all.'

Good. It would give her a chance to tell him that she wanted to cool their relationship. 'Could you man the fort for a few minutes so I could go and see Mabel on my way back? I want her to know the cat's all right.'

'Sure. If it stays quiet I'll be in my office.'

'Right.'

She went up to the geriatric ward and found a nurse.

'I'm looking for my neighbour—Mabel? She was admitted last night with a head injury.'

'Oh, yes, Mabel Walsh. She's over here. She's got another neighbour with her—Dora?'

'Oh, yes, I met her last night. Well, I won't stay long.'

'I'm sure she'll be pleased to see you, but she can't speak, of course. She's getting awfully agitated about something but we can't communicate with her. We've tried everything. Here she is. Look, Mabel, a visitor for you!'

Mabel reached out with her left hand and clutched at

Ginny's fingers. Her mouth worked, but nothing came out, and her face collapsed and the tears ran down her crumpled cheeks.

'Hello, sweetheart,' Ginny said gently, and perched on the edge of the bed. 'What's the matter? They tell me you've been upset about something. Is it the cat? Are you worried about him?'

She nodded, sort of, and relief lit her features. Ginny smiled. 'I knew you would be because I know how much you love him. He's fine. He's eating me out of house and home; he slept on my bed last night and he's disgustingly contented. I tell you what, I'll ask the ward nurse if I can bring him in to see you, shall I? I'm sure you'd both like that. Perhaps tomorrow?'

'Oh, it is,' Mabel said. Ginny was sure it wasn't what she'd wanted to say but it was the best she could achieve, and Ginny understood. She kissed her cheek.

'Don't worry about anything. Dora will look after the house, I'll look after the cat and you just get better.'

She went down to A and E, glad she'd made the effort to visit Geronimo's owner and set her mind at rest and pleased with her idea of taking the cat in. It was no use asking the night staff. She'd ring the day nurse in the morning.

And now, she thought unhappily, she had to deal with Ryan.

However, he had his own agenda. He drew her into his office, shut the door and stood looking at her, his lovely green eyes concerned. 'Virginia, I want to talk to you about last night,' he began. 'You left so suddenly—was it because of Ann?'

'I don't belong there, O'Connor,' she told him softly. 'I'm not your wife, I'm not their mother. I'm not anybody's mother, and I'm not going to be.'

'That doesn't mean you don't have a place there with me, Virginia. It can be a different place.'

'It is a different place.'

'Not your Category Three again,' he growled.

'It's what we agreed. No strings, no involvement—just an affair. Isn't that what you said?'

His eyes searched hers. 'Can't I change my mind?'

She looked away, unable to believe the message in them. He wasn't falling in love with her. He might think he was, but when he realised—when the crunch came— that was a whole new ball game.

And she couldn't bring herself to tell him—to ruin what little they had, to take away the joy she found with him. It was cowardly but, so long as she kept their relationship in perspective and didn't allow herself to grow too fond of the children, how could it hurt?

So, instead of the words she had meant to say, she let him draw her into his arms and kiss her, and she kissed him back, and she never actually answered his question because there was a knock on the door and all hell broke loose again, and it was the last time that night that they had more than two seconds to rub together.

Things were just steadily hectic until a little after midnight, but then a young man came into the department, looking very distressed.

'Um—we've got Buzz in the car—she's gone all funny—don't know what's wrong with her. I think she's passed out.'

Ginny called for help and went out to the car. A girl of about eighteen was sprawled across the laps of two others in the back of a battered old banger, and Ginny could see from a quick glance that she was unconscious.

'Right, let's get her out and into the light and see what's wrong. Anybody got any ideas what may have happened?'

She looked around the car, and sighed inwardly. They were all obviously as high as kites, but on what? And had Buzz, or whatever her name was, taken the same thing?

Or things. They pulled her out of the car, lifted her onto a trolley and took her inside. Once there they could see that she was deeply unconscious and unresponsive.

Ginny turned to the nurse working with her. 'Could you get Ryan for me? He's gone back to his room.'

She checked the girl's blood pressure and found that it was high but at least her breathing was still normal, although a little depressed. 'OK, I want to know everything you can tell me,' she said to the cluster of Buzz's friends. 'What's she had, when did you notice anything wrong, any strange behaviour, anything at all you think might be relevant?'

The lad who had come in first of all shrugged and gestured helplessly. 'Could be anything, man. She'll do anything she can get, know what I mean? She's crazy. That's why we call her Buzz. She does E and speed and acid—hell, man, there was so much going down tonight. People were getting off on everything.'

Helpful, Ginny thought. She looked round the group. 'Anybody else got any ideas?'

They shook their heads, but one girl was chewing her lip and looked very shifty.

Ginny looked directly at her. 'Have you got any ideas? Without help she could die, and we need to know exactly what she's had. If you know, you have to tell us.'

The girl shrugged. 'She might have had Es—I saw her buy something off this guy—I know he deals.'

Ryan arrived, coming into view behind the group.

'Problems?' he said over her shoulder.

'Drugs, we think. Not sure what—possibly Ecstasy or a cocktail.'

'Right. If you could go with this nurse, all of you, and tell her everything you know—Jen, report back to us with anything constructive ASAP, please?' He dumped his coat, shoved up his sleeves and pulled on gloves.

'Treat as for HIV,' he reminded her. 'Right, how deep is she?'

'I haven't had time to check on the Glasgow coma scale, but pretty deep.'

'Any gag reflex?'

She shook her head. 'I don't think so. We need to pump her out.'

'Yeah. Right, let's have her in Resus and get a cuffed tube in, then find out what's in her stomach. She needs an IV line with five per cent dextrose, and we need to get on to Toxicology to find out what we do next, but she looks to me as if she's got a raised intracranial pressure, which is typical of Ecstasy. They drink too much, their kidneys pack up and they get hyperhydrated. What's her pulse?'

'Slow and bounding.'

'Damn. OK, let's move.'

They got the tube in, pumped her stomach out and found the remnants of some white tablets. No food, which was typical of habitual speed users and probably why she was so thin.

The others were too, and their eyes were wild and they were all talking a mile a minute. Even in there they could hear them.

'High as kites,' Ryan said bitterly. 'Look at her. We need to admit her to ITU for really intensive supervision. I'm not at all happy about that intracranial pressure—I'm sure her brain's turning into a soggy sponge. She needs that pressure monitored, dialysis and probably something to strip that water out of her brain, but it needs a renal specialist or toxicologist. Who is she, do we know? Or is Buzz as good as it gets?

'I think we need the police in here to talk to this lot and find out who sold this kid whatever rubbish she's had. I'll get on that now, if you could ring ITU and tell them to stand by for her.'

Buzz was taken up to ITU immediately, even though ITU were pushed for nursing cover, because of the seriousness of her condition. One of the others in the group was starting to look a bit odd and went into a seizure, and, by the time the police arrived and Ryan had laid it on the line about how sick Buzz and their other friend was, they were all thoroughly rattled and were prepared to tell the police and Ryan all they knew.

It was three a.m. before they all left to go down to the police station, and they were still no nearer to knowing who Buzz really was or who might be worried about her.

'How can parents let their children get mixed up with such influences?' Ryan said angrily. 'She's just a kid.'

'There are bad kids as well as good kids, O'Connor,' Ginny reminded him. 'Maybe she's one of the bad influences? It doesn't sound as if you need to go out of your way to get hold of drugs at these events. Anyway, it's the pushers you want to get angry with, not the kids,' she added.

'Yes, and if I had my way, hanging would be too good for them. They're the scum of the earth.'

Oh, yes. Ginny poured a cup of coffee and handed it to him, her hands trembling. 'Do you think she'll make it?'

He rammed his hands through his hair. 'I don't know. Maybe. If her condition can be reversed quickly, then perhaps she'll recover. Maybe she'll be sufficiently scared to lay off drugs now before she ruins her life—if it's not too late.'

'If.' Ginny cradled her cup of coffee and tried to keep the shivers at bay. If, she thought. If only.

She had good reason to regret her only experiment with drugs. She'd been seventeen, easily led and had been offered cannabis at a party. It had been on the way back, with the driver high as a kite from a cocktail supplied by an unscrupulous pusher, that they'd left the road and she'd been impaled on the bridge railings.

Funny, she thought, apart from the scars she seemed fine, and yet she wasn't and never would be. All for a few minutes of idle curiosity...

CHAPTER SEVEN

GINNY's first job in the morning, after a few minutes taken to clean herself up and have breakfast, was to contact the day sister on the geriatric ward and ask if she could take the cat in to visit Mabel.

'Oh, what a lovely idea. She'd be thrilled, I'm sure. She's so dreadfully depressed, poor love. It must be hell not being able to communicate.'

So into her busy schedule she packed a trip home at lunchtime to take Geronimo in to the ward. It was a huge success. She'd tied a bit of string to his collar just in case he tried to do a runner, but he walked up Mabel's chest, nuzzled her with his head and settled down with his paws folded and dribbled ecstatically all over her front.

Predictably, Mabel cried, fondling the cat with her one functioning hand, and Ginny sat beside them holding the other end of the string and thought how glad she was that she'd thought of it. All too soon, though, it was time to take him back, and she promised Mabel that she'd bring him in again.

She got back to A and E to find a couple of reporters there waiting to speak to her. 'Why me and what about?' she asked the receptionist.

'Something about last night? Some girl in ITU with Ecstasy problems?'

'Oh, Lord,' she muttered, and went to find Ryan. 'The newshounds are after us—they've heard about Buzz.'

'Oh, hell. I don't have time. Tell them we can't comment.'

She did, but they were unwilling to give up. It was hot news—there'd been a lot of publicity, several young people had died in recent months and they wanted their story.

'All I can tell you is she's receiving the best possible care, and she's no longer in our hands here in this department,' she told them.

'But you admitted her. Was she conscious?'

'What about the others?'

'Who sold her the drugs?'

The questions were thick and fast, and she had no answers.

'I'm sorry, I can't answer that. You'll have to excuse me, I've got work to do,' she told them.

'Have you any comment to make about the people who sell the drugs to these kids?' one desperate reporter got in finally.

She turned back to them. 'Yes, I have. They're scum. The lowest of the low. They cause so much grief and heartache and distress—nothing the courts can do to them is severe enough.'

And with that she turned away.

She was quoted, of course, all over the late edition of the evening paper. Ryan turned up with a copy in his hand at eight o'clock, just as she was about to fall into bed for an early night after the hectic night on duty.

'Have you seen this?' he demanded, brandishing the paper at her.

'No. May I?'

'"SCUM PUSHERS THE LOWEST OF THE LOW",' he read, and handed it to her. She scanned it quickly.

'Oh, blast. Well, at least they didn't misquote me.'

'I thought I told you not to comment?'

'I didn't—not on Buzz. Just on pushers.'

'Oh, well, at least you didn't say taking Ecstasy was

normally harmless and all kids indulged in drugs and it was just unfortunate, which is what all the stars seem to be saying about these unlucky kids. How are they expected to know the truth if their idols lie to them?'

He threw the paper aside and gave her a tentative smile. 'Are you just off to bed?'

Heaven help her, she loved him. She let an inviting smile curve her lips. 'Yes, I was. Want to join me for a while?'

'I thought you'd never ask,' he murmured, and his hand reached out to her, drawing her close.

'Aren't you tired?' she asked, her hands resting on his broad, firm shoulders.

'Shattered. I still need you. I don't think I could ever be too tired to hold you in my arms.'

She reached up, threaded her fingers through his hair and pulled his head down to hers. His lips were hard and hungry, his body instantly responding to the contact, and she forgot all the reasons why this wasn't a good idea and why she wanted to keep her distance, forgot that she was supposed to be keeping their relationship in perspective, and gave herself up to his loving without a second's hesitation.

She loved him, he needed her—there was no other truth. To hell with tomorrow.

'We're going to a horse show near us tomorrow,' he told her on Friday. 'The kids say they want to go, and there'll be a dog show on the site as well—it might be quite fun, if you can stand the animals.'

She laughed. 'I love animals; of course I'll come,' she told him, and forgot that she was supposed to be keeping her distance from the kids, forgot that she wasn't allowed to play happy families with him and his children, forgot all the things she'd sworn she'd remember. He only had to look at her, touch her with those expressive green eyes, and she'd forget her own name.

She could even forget the very reason why she had to remember.

They picked her up on Saturday morning at ten thirty. Evie was looking mutinous in the back, and Ryan winked at Ginny.

'She wanted to go first thing. She'd heard it started at eight, and she wanted to be there. I told her no. Boy, can that little girl throw a tantrum when it suits her!'

'She's just testing you,' Ginny said.

'Well, she found out what I was made of, that's for sure.' He opened the door for her and helped her in, lingering unnecessarily over the seat belt so that she pushed him away and met his twinkling eyes with a repressive glare.

At least it was meant to be, but he was so full of himself that it was like water off a duck's back, and she ended up smiling and letting him fasten her seat belt, carefully adjusting it so that it lay just so over her bust.

'O'Connor!' she said warningly in an undertone.

He grinned, quite unabashed, ran his knuckles over the swell of her breasts under the edge of her blouse and closed her door, swaggering round to the driver's side and whistling merrily. He looked disgustingly pleased with himself, and she had to smile. Idiot, she thought fondly, and her heart contracted. Oh, how she loved him. How she loved all of them.

If only there was a chance for them, but there wasn't. She wasn't wife material. She knew that. She was a quick study and didn't need to be told a thing more than once.

They arrived at the showground and Evie forgot her

sulks instantly because the first thing they saw when they got out of the car was an ice-cream van.

'Oh, Daddy, please,' she pleaded, her stomach upset clearly forgotten. Gus, too, was clamouring, and Ryan ended up buying four ice creams, one for each of them, and then—because there were a lot of big horses about and he was worried about the children getting trampled—he put Gus on his shoulders and Ginny took Evie by the hand, and they wandered round together.

'That's a big horse,' Evie said, with eyes like saucers, as a magnificent chestnut gelding trotted past them on his way to the ring.

Ryan looked up and agreed with her. 'He certainly is. Quite a handful, too, for that lady. She doesn't look as if she can quite control him.'

The chestnut was pulling a little—even Ginny could see that—and the woman was having trouble getting him to settle down. She took him into the warm-up arena, and he seemed to be rushing the jumps a little, Ginny thought. She turned to Ryan.

'Do you know anything about horses?' she asked him.

'Yes—quite a bit. My parents had a ranch. I grew up riding, out of necessity. He's too much for her; whatever is she thinking about?'

'She looks pale,' Ginny said thoughtfully. 'Do you suppose she's all right?'

'Probably scared half to death. Most women who ride big horses like to be terrified. That's why they do it.'

The horse seemed to settle down then, and they watched the others as they competed in turn in the ring. The jumps were all natural-coloured logs and poles, with bits of brush and tree—unlike the coloured poles in the other ring—and they learned that this was the working hunter class.

The jumps looked huge, that was all Ginny knew, and

Evie and Gus watched in fascination as the horses went over the big obstacles.

Then the chestnut came in, all sweated up and keen, and Ryan looked at the woman on him and frowned. 'I think you're right. She doesn't look too good. Perhaps she's ill.'

She was, or so it transpired. The first jump was all right, and the second, but as the horse jumped the third he began to accelerate and just before the fourth the rider seemed to sag onto his neck.

He went over the jump at a flat-out gallop, turned sharply left and, like a rag doll, the rider toppled off and rolled straight towards them.

Ryan muttered something, hoisted Gus off his shoulders, set him down by Ginny and ran over to the woman, arriving as the Red Cross official did.

'I'm a doctor,' Ginny heard Ryan say, and she watched helplessly as he checked the woman's airway, cupping a hand under her neck to check for spinal injuries and support her until the rigid collar could be applied. The woman standing beside Ginny was clearly concerned.

'Do you suppose we should do anything?' she said to Ginny.

'I'm a doctor too—if you'd be kind enough to look after the children, I could go and help.'

She handed them over and ran across to Ryan.

'What can I do?'

'Check her spine. She's breathing, but she's hellish hot and she's out cold.'

'She must be concussed,' the Red Cross man was saying.

Ryan shook his head. 'No, she passed out on the horse. I was watching her. I don't think she's got a head injury, but she might well have hurt herself in the fall.'

Ginny was feeling down the patient's spine, joint by

joint, looking for any irregularity or swelling, but there was nothing obvious. 'If she's got a fracture, it's not displaced,' she told Ryan. 'I'll check her legs.'

'Her pupils are reacting,' he murmured. 'I think she might be coming round.'

He took the girl's hand. 'Hello there. Can you hear me? I'm a doctor. Can you tell me what happened?'

Her eyes blinked open and filled with tears. 'My back,' she whispered raggedly. 'I hurt...'

He smoothed her hair off her face and tried again. 'Can you tell me your name?'

'Debbie,' she croaked. 'Debbie McNab. Where am I?'

'You've had a fall. Can you tell me what happened?'

'Her legs seem all right,' Ginny said softly.

'Thanks. Any idea?'

She shook her head, and Ryan glanced at Ginny. 'Neck movement seems free enough. I think we'll have a collar on just to be on the safe side. Debbie, have you had a cold or anything recently?'

She nodded, her eyes filling again. 'My head hurts,' she whispered, and promptly retched.

Ryan let her settle again, then said, 'Tell me about your cold.'

'Flu,' she corrected tearfully. 'I feel awful. Where am I?'

'You fell off your horse,' Ryan told her.

'Oh. Where is he?'

Ginny looked around. 'Someone's caught him.'

Debbie looked puzzled.

'He's all right,' Ginny assured her, and a voice in the crowd confirmed that the horse would be taken care of.

'Oh.' Her eyes slid shut, but Ryan wouldn't let her sleep.

'Wake up, Debbie. Come on. Let's put this collar on

you and get you into the ambulance. Backboard as well, please.'

She was rolled to the side, then rolled back onto the board and her head taped in position. Ryan had taken her hat off very carefully, but there was no sign of injury to her head apart from a slight bruise.

'Is anybody here with her?' he asked, looking around.

'I am,' a woman in the crowd said.

'Can we contact her family? Husband or partner?'

'Her husband—leave that with us, we'll get hold of him. Is she all right?'

'I think so,' Ryan said. 'She'd better go to hospital just to be on the safe side. It was a nasty fall. Was she ill this morning?'

'Yes—I kept telling her she shouldn't do it, but she insisted. She hasn't got a spleen, by the way. I don't know if that's relevant. She lost it after another riding accident.'

Ryan looked grim, Ginny thought, as they lifted Debbie onto the stretcher and into the ambulance. He followed her in to give her a more thorough examination in the privacy of the ambulance, and Ginny went back to the children.

The woman in the crowd who had spoken to them turned to Ginny. 'She will be all right, won't she? I didn't see her fall. She's usually such a good rider, but everyone said she was all over the place.'

'She passed out before she fell. It must be the flu. Yes, I think she'll be all right, but she ought to go and have some X-rays and just make sure. Are you happy to contact her husband?'

'Yes—and my partner can sort out the horse and get the lorry taken back to her yard. Thanks for helping.'

Ginny smiled. 'It's a pleasure. It makes a change to be on the spot. Usually we just get the results, not the action!'

She went back to the children, who were wide eyed and excited. 'Is Daddy going in the ambulance?' Evie asked.

'I don't know. We'll have to wait and find out.'

He emerged then, and came over to them. 'I'm going with her to the hospital—can you manage to drive my car and follow?'

'Oh, Daddy, we don't want to leave!' Evie wailed.

'You could always take my keys and bring my car back here,' Ginny suggested.

'Do you mind? What about insurance?'

She grinned. 'You over twenty-five?'

He laughed. 'Only by ten years,' he said drily. 'Keys?'

She fished in her pocket, pulled out the keys and handed them to him. 'Don't worry about us. There's a man over there selling chips and hot dogs. We'll be fine. See you later.'

He kissed her cheek and ran, leaving her with the children staring up at her optimistically.

'Can we have chips?' Gus asked.

'If you promise not to be sick—but no green lollies, no popcorn and not too much ketchup.'

'He always has too much ketchup,' Evie said with authority. 'Can we find some little ponies to watch afterwards? I don't like the big horses, they're scary.'

Ginny was inclined to agree with her so, after they had queued for their chips and hot dogs, they went over to another little ring where there were some pretty little ponies being led round, their manes and tails silky and their coats gleaming in the sun. They settled themselves and watched the much more sedate event from the comfort of a patch of grassy shade.

The pony who won was a pretty little Shetland, a real Thelwell pony with a flowing black mane and tail, and as he trotted past them sporting his red rosette Evie sighed longingly.

'I want a pony like that,' she said wistfully, 'but Daddy says no.'

And after watching that fall, Ginny didn't suppose that he was any more likely to change his mind! 'How about an ice cream?' she suggested, navigating them away from the dangerous reefs of these uncharted waters.

'What, instead of a pony?' Evie said with a grin.

Ginny laughed and got to her feet. 'Silly. Come on, Angus, let's go and find something else to eat.'

They were on their way over to the ice-cream van when they found someone offering pony rides for charity.

'Oh, please, can I have a go?' Evie begged.

Ginny was tempted, but without Ryan's permission she felt it wasn't a good idea. The ponies looked quiet enough, but Evie wasn't her child and the decision wasn't hers to make.

'Let's wait for Daddy,' she suggested, and then as if Evie had spirited him out of thin air he was there, and she was running towards him to grab his hand and work her charms on him.

'All right, then, if you must,' he said with an indulgent smile, and he paid for both children and watched as their hats were fitted and they were led off down the field.

'How's the patient?' Ginny asked him.

'Oh, OK. She's feeling pretty rough, but I think that's the flu as much as anything. Her husband turned up and Jack was there, so I left them to it.' He took her hand and put her keys into it, lingering over the contact. 'Kids been all right?'

'Yes, fine. We watched some little ponies.' She met his eyes. 'Evie wants one.'

He groaned. 'Tell me about it. We just can't take on

that sort of commitment and, anyway, she's far too young. She can have riding lessons later when she's older, and if she's really keen she can have a pony then. For now, though, I'd just as soon keep her safe.'

Ginny chuckled. 'Now how did I know you'd say that?' she said with a smile.

'You ought to try being a parent one day,' he groaned.

Ginny felt as if she'd been gutted. If only, she thought. She turned away, her eyes stinging and her throat clogged with unshed tears. Oh, God, if only…

The children came back then, chattering like magpies, and she was able to get herself under control while they bounced around their father and told him what their ponies had been called and how lovely they were and how they wanted another ride—of course.

Ryan shook his head. 'I've got a surprise for you—I bumped into Jilly and Zach at the hospital, and they said did we want to go over and have a barbeque this afternoon?'

'With Scud?' Gus squeaked. 'Oh, Daddy, yes!'

'Are we going?' Evie said, the pony rides forgotten.

'If Virginia wants to,' he told them, looking up and meeting her eyes.

'Am I invited?' she said quietly, suddenly uncertain.

'Of course. I told them you were spending the day with us.'

'Then, yes, I'd love to,' she said with a smile. 'It sounds fun.'

It was fun—if one didn't mind being interrogated just the teeniest bit! They were both obviously curious about her relationship with Ryan, not so much the fact of it but the direction.

And that was one thing she wanted clear from the start.

'Don't start getting ideas about us,' she said to Jilly while Ryan and Zach and the children were chasing Scud round the field. 'There's no future in it. We both went into it knowing that. I'd just hate you to get the wrong idea and say something in front of the children because if there's one thing I can't do it's take their mother's place. Ryan's made it more than clear that I'm not in line for Ann's job. I think he's still in love with her, anyway. It's only been a fairly short while.'

Jilly looked at her in puzzlement. 'But he loves you, Ginny! Anyone could see it.'

She shook her head. 'No. He wants me. It's different. It's just been a long time for him and he's letting himself go and having fun. One day he'll wake up and look at me and realise I'm not what he thought I was, and that will be that. Until then, well...' she lifted her shoulders in an eloquent shrug '...I'll take each day and be thankful for it.'

Jilly stared at her. 'Do you know, I would have thought you'd be brimful of confidence, looking as you do, but you're not, are you? You've got no idea of your own worth.'

Ginny laughed softly, but it was a cold, empty sound. 'Oh, I know. I'm just a mistress, Jill. Not a wife.'

The men came back over then, throwing themselves down on the ground and gasping for breath. Evie and Gus ran after them and sat on them, one on each chest—which did nothing for the men's breathing—and laughed delightedly.

'You're all hot,' Gus said, patting his father's cheek.

'So are you,' he groaned, and shifted the boy off onto the grass.

Evie stayed where she was on Zach's chest, bouncing for added effect, and laughing when he went, 'Oof.'

'Good practice for you,' Jilly said. 'You've only got until February—you've got a lot to learn.'

Zach groaned and rolled over, taking Evie with him into a giggling heap on the grass. He tickled her until she begged for mercy, and eventually let her go. 'I tell you what, who wants to come and see Scud's puppies?' he said casually.

The children leapt up and squealed with delight, and dragged Ryan to his feet.

'Come on, Daddy, you have to come,' they begged.

Then Evie turned to Ginny and grabbed her hand. 'Come on, Ginny, you too!' she said, her eyes sparkling and her hair flying. Laughing, to cover the sudden surge of love that left her weak with longing, Ginny scrambled to her feet and took the proffered hand.

'Come on, then. Let's go and see these puppies.' She looked across to Jilly. 'You coming?'

The other woman shook her head, her eyes on Ginny, missing nothing. And in those eyes Ginny herself could read compassion.

She looked away. She didn't need sympathy. She wasn't strong enough to handle it, not by a country mile.

'I'll stay and get the food on,' Jilly was saying. 'Don't be too long.'

They were ages. The puppies, of course, were wonderful. Fat, squiggling bundles of black with stubby legs and bright pink tongues and teeth like needles, they were a delight. Ginny sat on the kitchen floor of the nearby farmhouse and they climbed all over her—chewing the laces of her trainers, wobbling along her legs and falling off in little heaps—while their mother watched indulgently from the sidelines.

One graced her thigh with a little puddle, but she didn't

care. They were so delicious she could forgive them anything.

'This is the one we're having,' Zach said, holding up
one of the bigger male puppies. 'We haven't got a name
for him yet—he's just Junior. He's just like Scud was as
a pup, apparently.'

'Two like him?' Ryan said with a groan. 'You must like
punishment.'

'It's Jilly that'll have the problem. She's the one who'll
be at home with them both.'

'I don't suppose you want one, do you?' the farmer's
wife said hopefully.

Evie and Gus immediately started clamouring, but Ryan
was adamant. 'We'll borrow Scud and Junior sometimes,'
he promised, 'but it's not fair to have a dog when I'm out
at work all day.'

Evie's face fell. 'If we had a mummy we could have a
dog,' she said mournfully.

Ryan's eyes closed briefly. 'Come on, sweetheart,' he
said gently. 'Give Junior one last hug and let's go back—
supper must be nearly ready now.'

Ginny stood up carefully, lowering one particularly am-
bitious mountaineer to the ground by her mother. Evie
kissed Junior on the nose, then put him down beside his
sisters and brothers and slipped her hand into Ginny's.

'Can I walk with you?' she asked wistfully.

Ginny's heart did a funny little somersault. 'Of course,
darling,' she said, taking the little hand firmly in hers and
squeezing it. 'Shall we see how many steps it takes to get
back to Jilly?'

It was nearly six hundred—nearly long enough to get
her emotions under control again. Six thousand might have
been better, but just walking along with that trusting little

hand in hers made the emotional progress infinitely slower. In fact, Ginny thought, six million might not have been enough because it was Evie who was tearing her apart.

She would have gone, then, run away, but her car was back at Ryan's where they'd left it to save both of them driving out to Zach's, and she was trapped with him.

So she put on a brave face that fooled everybody except Jill, and carried on as if nothing had happened. It seemed to take an interminable time for everybody to eat, she thought. They all munched away and chattered and laughed, and she thought her face would crack and fall to pieces by the time Ryan finally rounded up the children and they said their goodbyes.

The children were tired out after all the dashing around with Scud, and they were quiet in the car.

'Come in and have a drink,' Ryan suggested, but it was more than she could bear—to go back into his house and sit in the room with his wife's photo and smile for so much as another minute.

'I won't,' she told him, using the cat as an excuse. 'Anyway, I ought to go and visit Mabel tonight. I haven't seen her since Friday morning.'

She left the moment they arrived back—or would have if Evie hadn't run up to the car just as she was about to close the door.

'Goodbye, Ginny,' she said sweetly. 'Thank you for spending the day with us.'

And she leant into the car and kissed Ginny's cheek, before darting away to her father and waving brightly.

Ginny waved back, and then started the engine and drove away, leaving part of her heart behind.

*   *   *

'She looked sad tonight, Daddy,' Evie said as he tucked her up.

'I know,' Ryan agreed. 'I wonder what was the matter. Perhaps she was just tired.'

'But she looked *sad*,' Evie insisted.

Ryan had noticed. He had been thinking about little else. She often looked sad, he thought, and wondered again if she would ever trust him enough to tell him what had put that haunted look in her eyes.

'I wish she could be our new mummy,' Evie said slowly.

Ryan's gut clenched. A new mummy? he thought. Virginia, here with them all the time, doing the things a mother did?

To his surprise it sounded wonderful. Not at all wrong, or hasty, or unseemly—but absolutely, entirely, naturally right. Would it work, though? Would she want to take on someone else's children?

She was terrific with them, that was for sure. She seemed to have an instinct for dealing with them that he envied at times, and she had an easy affection that didn't threaten their mother's memory but lay alongside it, giving an added warmth.

Yes, they'd be safe with her, he thought. She'd be kind and fair, and there would be others too—little replicas of her with her dark brown hair and cloud-grey eyes and generous, smiling mouth.

It was a theory he was warming to rapidly, he realised. Very rapidly indeed...

CHAPTER EIGHT

GINNY arrived home with a few tins of cat food bought at a late-night corner shop, and found a note through her door. It was written in a quavering script and, before she read it, Ginny knew what it would say. It was from Dora, Mabel Walsh's next-door neighbour, and was brief and to the point.

'Sorry to say Mabel died this afternoon.'

It was the last straw. She let herself in, sat down on the sofa with Geronimo on her lap and cried her eyes out.

He thought that was the giddy limit, and went and sat in the kitchen by the fridge and yammered at her until she pulled herself together and went and fed him. 'I guess you're mine now, old son,' she said heavily. 'Oh, well, at least I'm not alone.'

Self-pity, she thought to herself as she mopped up another spate of tears, was a disgusting indulgence. It was on a par with eating too many chocolates and allowing herself the luxury of an affair with Ryan.

The phone rang, and she answered it absently.

'Hi,' he murmured, his voice soft and husky. 'What are you doing?'

She swallowed the last of her tears. 'Missing you,' she said, because she couldn't bring herself to be cheerful and lie.

She could hear his concern almost before he spoke. 'Virginia, are you all right?'

She sighed heavily. 'I will be. My neighbour died this

afternoon, apparently. Geronimo's owner. I think I might
have inherited him.'

'Oh, Virginia, I'm sorry. Do you want me to come
over?'

'What for?' she said. 'It's not as if I knew her.'

'You just sound upset.'

'Do I? Don't worry. It's just reaction.'

There was a silence. 'Honey, are you sure everything's
all right?' he said cautiously.

His concern was nearly her undoing. No, she wanted to
scream, it's not all right and it never will be, and I want
you to hold me and tell me you love me anyway, but you
won't because I can't tell you because I can't bear to see
the look on your face—

'Of course everything's all right,' she said brightly,
changing the subject. 'We had a good day today, didn't
we? The kids seemed to enjoy themselves.'

'Yes, they did. Thanks for looking after them while I
went with that girl to the hospital.'

'It was a pleasure, they were no trouble. I wonder how
she is?'

'She's OK—I rang. They've discharged her—reluctantly—because her husband said he'd look after her and
make sure she was all right, and the worst thing wrong
with her was flu and she's probably better off at home
asleep.'

'Are they happy that she didn't have a head injury?'

'Seem to be. Jack wouldn't have let her go otherwise.'
There was a pause, then he said, 'Evie missed you tonight
for her bedtime story. We finished *Black Beauty*—she said
you would have loved the ending. She wants you to read
it to her again some time, and Gus said you hadn't read
to him yet and he wanted you to next time you were
round.'

Ginny was choked. They were sucking her in, with or without her permission. Did she dare to let them? What if it all fell apart? She couldn't take it again, there was so much more to lose this time—

'Look, I have to go. This cat needs to go out and I ought to sort out somewhere more permanent for him to sleep. He's decided he likes being on the bed with me.'

'Sensible cat,' Ryan said huskily. 'Do you suppose he wants to swap with me for a couple of hours? I could ask Suzannah to pop over—I'm sure she'd be happy to.'

Ginny was tempted. Desperately tempted, but her emotions were too fragile at that moment to cope with Ryan in a sexy, romantic mood. One caress from those sensuous, sympathetic green eyes and she'd turn into a watering-can again.

'Take a hike, O'Connor,' she told him drily. 'All you think about is your hormones.'

'It's you,' he murmured. 'You do things to me that wreck my self-control. I used to be a good boy.'

'You still are good.' She chuckled.

He laughed softly. 'It's kind of you to say so. You're pretty damn fine yourself, lady.' His voice changed, deepening. 'Lord, Virginia, I want you. Why the hell aren't you here with me?'

'Because you told your mother-in-law no hanky-panky,' she reminded him.

'Is that why you left so early?'

'You know why I left so early,' she lied, changing tack. 'I was going to see Mabel. Now I have to sort out this cat of hers and make sure he's not emotionally scarred by the experience. I'll see you on Monday.'

'What about tomorrow?'

'I'm on duty tomorrow.'

'Oh. Damn. OK. Well, take care. We'll miss you.' And finally he let her hang up.

The cat needed no sorting out. He was sorted, curled up in the middle of her bed, perfectly content. Emotionally scarred, my eye, she thought drily, climbing into the bed a few minutes later. 'Shove up, you,' she said, pushing him gently with her foot.

He grumbled but settled down again a few inches to the right, and she lay there and thought of Ryan and his children and how if the world was less perverse she might be there with them, and when the cat came up to the top of the bed and pushed his face into hers in greeting she turned on her side, draped an arm over him and fell asleep with the contented rumble of his purr in her ear, only too glad not to be completely alone.

She was glad to be at work the following day. It took her mind off Ryan—at least until she had time to sit down and share a cup of coffee with Patrick Haddon. She was on duty with him for the day, and he gave her the news that Buzz, their junkie teenager, was making good progress. 'She seems to have made a good recovery, thanks to all the attention she got. I don't know, kids these days seem to get into all sorts of trouble. It wasn't like that when we were young.'

'Wasn't it?' Ginny said sceptically. 'I seem to remember some fairly hairy goings-on in my youth.'

'You must have had a less sheltered upbringing than me,' Patrick said with a laugh. 'I got skinned alive by my father if I came in smelling of cider!'

'Oh, I got skinned alive, all right,' Ginny told him. 'Except for the one time when it all got a bit out of hand. Then they were only too glad that I *was* alive.'

Patrick put his feet up on the coffee-table and balanced

his mug on his belt buckle. 'Sounds more exciting than my youth. Do tell.'

'Not exciting,' she corrected. 'Stupid, crazy, terrifying. I went to a party with a boy I hardly knew, he overstepped the mark with some drugs; someone spiked his drink and I didn't notice or care because I was busy conducting my one and only experiment with cannabis at the time.'

Patrick eyed her keenly. 'And?'

'He crashed the car. I got tangled up with some bridge railings. I was lucky to get away with it.'

'Ouch. Internal injuries?'

She smiled. 'Just a touch.'

'Spleen?'

She shook her head. 'No. Bowel mostly.' And the rest.

'You were lucky.'

'So they told me,' she replied cryptically. There was luck, though, and there was luck. Oh, yes. Lucky? Maybe.

'Lizzi Hamilton was lucky,' he was saying.

'Yes. How's she doing?'

'Oh, OK. Slowly but surely. Her legs were the worst worry in the end, and they seem to have lined up very well with surgery and are hopefully going to be fine. She'll be off her feet for a while, but I don't suppose they care about that. It's a small price to pay for being alive.'

Something in Patrick's voice alerted Ginny that there was more to follow, and she waited quietly, giving him time. 'Death's a funny old thing,' he said finally. 'I lost my first wife in an earthquake.'

'Oh, Patrick,' Ginny said, shocked despite the subtle warning. 'I'm so sorry, I didn't know. I had no idea you'd been married before.'

His smile was small and a little twisted. 'It was years ago now. We were in Mexico, in a little village. She was inside this school, and suddenly—without warning—there was an earth tremor and the school just folded up around her like a pack of cards. There was no hope of getting any of them out alive, but we tried anyway. The awful thing was that I never had the chance to say goodbye.'

He looked at his mug, studying it intently. 'That plagued me for years. It took a long time and a lot of patience from Anna before I really came to terms with losing Isobel.'

'I'm sure. It must be devastating.'

'It is. It was only finding Anna that really pulled me round and gave me the strength to go on. I don't know how Ryan's coped with it without anyone to support him through the worst of it. He's thousands of miles from his family.'

'No,' Ginny said surely. 'His family are with him. The children are his family.'

Patrick shook his head. 'Not in the way I mean. You can't unburden yourself to your children, especially not when they're so young. I'm not sure if having children makes it better or worse.'

'Better, I think. Otherwise there must be nothing left to show for it all. Also, I suppose because there are the children to consider you have to pull yourself together and get on with things, but on the other hand you have to deal with all their emotions as well, of course. It must be doubly hard if you're a man and expected to go out to work as well as run the home.'

'I think that helps,' Patrick told her. 'Without the support of my colleagues and a hectic schedule at work, I would have disappeared into a grey morass and never come out again.'

There was a bleak truth reflected in his mellow brown eyes, and Ginny wondered how badly Ann's death had really affected Ryan. Funny, she thought, they'd talked about the manner of her death, but never the impact it had made on them. On the subject of his period of grieving, Ryan had been utterly silent.

'How long's he been here?' she asked.

'Nearly two years now. She'd been dead about six months when he took the job.'

'And how was he?'

'Pretty rough. He hardly smiled, he did the job and went home, he never complained about anything—it was as if nothing mattered any more. Nothing was important enough to make any impression. It was quite hard to work with him at first but then gradually he began to relax and start to smile again, and just recently I've had the distinct impression he's lonely.'

Patrick shot her a grin. 'I guess that's where you came in. He's been much happier since you arrived, but that could be to do with hormones. It's amazing how frustration eats at your temper!'

Ginny blushed slightly, and he laughed. 'Sorry. I didn't mean to embarrass you, but you'd both have to be dead from the neck up if you weren't involved by now.'

'Involved?' she said with a little smile. 'Patrick, what can you mean?'

'You know what I mean. He is more relaxed, more contented. More reasonable! We're all grateful to you, actually. You're just what he needed.'

Patrick's words cheered her up a little. If she had eased Ryan's loneliness and made him happier, then perhaps she had contributed to his emotional recovery and set him on the road to a new life.

If that life couldn't be with her that didn't make her contribution any the less valuable.

Her contribution to the health of the local community picked up some momentum shortly after their conversation with a spate of weekend sporting injuries. The football season was getting under way, and it brought with it the predictable injuries of unused muscles suddenly overloaded and overstretched. They had a young lad with a hamstring injury, another with a torn thigh muscle and yet another with a broken ankle which had turned over on rough ground.

She passed Patrick in the corridor and showed him the X-ray. 'Another sportsman bites the dust,' she said with wry humour. 'I thought sport was supposed to be healthy?'

Patrick laughed. 'Whatever gave you that idea? I've just had a squash player who'll probably lose the sight of his eye after getting a ball in the socket. It was hard enough to give him a blow-out fracture of the orbital floor from the pressure, so I've admitted him for observation and investigation by the eye surgeon. I don't like the look of it at all.'

'How encouraging. Ryan and Zach play squash sometimes, I gather.'

'Mmm. I don't suppose they wear safety glasses either.'

'Shouldn't think so,' Ginny agreed. 'We all have this insane belief in our own immortality.'

'Not all of us,' Patrick said quietly. 'And losing that fundamental security can be a real threat to your sanity, if you let it.'

It was a sobering thought. Mabel had just died, presumably without expecting it. Ginny understood that Lizzi Hamilton's first husband had died, Patrick's first wife had died, Jack Lawrence had lost a son and Ann O'Connor had been snatched from her family in the prime of her life. It was a wonder anyone dared to go out.

The beast harvested where and when it suited him, she thought. And not only lives that were begun, but sometimes the potential—future lives, before the vital spark was even introduced.

Oh, yes. She knew all about that...

Ryan sought her out first thing on Monday morning, pulled her into his office and into his arms and did wonders for her melancholy.

'We missed you yesterday,' he said huskily, nuzzling her neck. 'Lord, Virginia, you feel good.'

She chuckled. 'Just at the moment I feel distinctly naughty,' she teased.

He groaned and pulled her closer. 'Lunchtime,' he promised. 'We'll go and feed the cat.'

'He doesn't need feeding again.'

'So, who else knows that?' he said with a wicked grin.

She laughed. 'I hate to disillusion you, but if you think that telling everyone we're going to feed the cat will fool them for an instant you need your bumps felt.'

'So let them think what they like,' he said carelessly. 'We're all adults.'

'What they think,' she told him, 'is that I've done them all a favour because you're easier to live with now your hormones are getting exercised.'

He held her at arm's length. 'What? Who said that?'

'Patrick.'

He grinned lazily. 'Did he, indeed? Well, in that case he can cover for us while we go and exercise them some more!'

She slapped his wrist. 'Down, boy!' she told him. 'How can you expect me to work here with you carrying on like this every chance you get?'

'You'd be bored if I didn't,' he pointed out fairly, 'but you're probably right. I tell you what, how about coming over this evening and reading these kids their bedtime stories like I've promised them you will, and then we'll get

Suzannah to babysit them and I'll take you out to dinner? That suit your romantic little soul better?'

'And then what?' she said drily, not fooled for a moment.

His smile was slow, sensuous and did all sorts of funny things to her insides. 'Why, then I take you home, honey. What else?'

She laughed softly. 'What else, indeed.' Oh, Lord, it was tempting.

'Well?' he coaxed.

'Oh, I think I could probably manage that,' she submitted. 'On one condition.'

'Which is?'

'I don't have to read the whole of *Black Beauty* to Evie.'

He grinned. 'Well, not tonight, at least.'

She didn't. Only the last chapter, which made her go all sentimental and gooey, so that by the time Evie had slipped her little arms round Ginny's neck and kissed her, and Angus had snuggled against her for his own story and then coyly kissed her goodnight as well, she was mush.

They left as soon as Suzannah arrived, and Ryan took her to a new Italian restaurant and spoiled her. It was dark and intimate, made for lovers, and his knee was pressed against hers, his eyes locked with hers, one of his hands closed over one of hers—until she could hardly tell where she ended and he began.

His voice was soft and teasing and romantic, his eyes gleaming with promise in the flickering candlelight, and when they went back to her flat he turned her straight into his arms and kissed her ravenously.

There was no need for any preliminaries. They were both aching for each other after the slow, drawn-out intimacy of the restaurant and the enforced abstinence of the previous few days. They didn't even make it to the bed-room—well, at least, not the first time.

And when they did, they found Geronimo curled up in the middle of the bed.

He was most indignant to be evicted, but there was a time and a place for everything, Ryan said to him gently but firmly, and this was his time and his place, not the cat's.

'I do believe you're jealous,' Ginny teased, trailing a lazy finger over the centre of Ryan's bare, hair-scattered chest.

He trapped her hand in his. 'Too damn right I'm jeal-ous,' he growled. 'The cat gets to sleep with you. Do you realise I never have?'

'You're too old for sleep-over parties,' she told him, but it was true. They had never spent the night together, never spent more than a few hours together at a time and hardly ever alone. It was difficult with the children, too, because the only way they could snatch a night together would be if someone would look after them—someone like their grandmother?

She could just see Ryan convincing Betty and Doug to have the children for the weekend so that he could indulge himself with his mistress!

This time their love-making was slow and languid and tender, and afterwards Ryan seemed more thoughtful than usual. He held her close, his arms around her, and she could sense a deep frustration building up in him.

'I want to sleep with you,' he told her. 'We never have any time together alone. We're either working, entertaining the children or making love. There's no time to talk, to get to know each other. I know nothing about your life before you met me, really. Nothing at all.'

And what a good job, Ginny thought heavily, or he'd

be gone. 'I think we know each other pretty well,' she said evasively.

'I don't even know if you've got any family,' he said. 'Brothers, sisters, parents—I know nothing about them.'

'No brothers or sisters—just parents. They live quite near here.'

'I'd like to meet them,' he told her.

Funny, that. Her mother had said a very similar thing on the phone on Sunday. Her mouth ran away with her. 'Why don't we all go over there at the weekend?' she said rashly, and then could have bitten her tongue off. How on earth was that going to help any of them to remain uninvolved?

Ryan went very still, then turned towards her, searching her eyes. 'Really?'

And what could she say? No, I didn't mean it, my mouth was on autopilot?

'Really,' she confirmed. 'Of course,' she added hastily, clutching at straws, 'they might be busy.'

'Another time would do,' he mumbled, nuzzling the side of her neck. 'Virginia, what do you do to make yourself smell so good? I could just eat you—' He started to nibble her ear and she got the giggles, swatting him away, and the problem of her parents was forgotten for the time.

He pinned her down and she struggled, pushing him over onto his back and sitting astride his chest, his hands shackled together over his head. 'There,' she said in satisfaction. 'Get out of that, O'Connor.'

He lay there, a smile on his face that would have fitted the Cheshire cat. 'Maybe I don't want to,' he said.

She gave a sensuous little laugh. 'Maybe you can't.'

He pulled his hands away from hers effortlessly, seized her hips and slid her down his body until she was neatly positioned—and very much aware.

'Can't I?' he teased.

Her eyes flew open wide. 'How on earth did you manage that?'

He gave her an innocent look. 'I can't imagine. It just seems to happen every time I'm near you.'

She shifted slightly, dragging a groan from his chest. 'Now you've got me where you want me, what are you going to do with me?' he said huskily.

She glanced at the bedside clock. 'Nothing. It's nearly midnight. Suzannah's got college tomorrow. Get up.'

'I have,' he said wickedly.

She smacked his shoulder lightly and rolled away. 'Behave. How can I take you to meet my mother when you're so bad?'

'I thought you said I was good?' he teased, stretching lazily.

She gave up. He was too inviting, too big and male and sensuously overloading for her to stand a chance of winning against her instincts—and he would be home only a *little* after midnight!

It was a whole eight hours before she saw him again, and he was every bit as distractingly gorgeous as he had been the night before. They were busy, though, so she only had time to snatch a cup of coffee with him mid-morning.

'About the weekend,' he said. 'We haven't got any commitments either day so we can fit in with whatever your mother wants, if you're sure she can be bothered.'

'Of course she can be bothered,' Ginny said honestly. Her mother had been nagging to meet him for weeks, to her abject horror. Not that she was worried about her mother. Her mother had the tact of a diplomat. It was her father who waded in with concrete wellies on.

Oh, well. She'd just have to keep them all apart, she

thought, and then didn't have time to worry about it any more because it all got rather hectic again.

She spent the day poking and prodding and retrieving fish bones, and she was actually quite relieved when a more seriously injured patient was admitted.

Not that it was good news for the patient. A man in his thirties, he had been innocently walking his dog when a big four-wheel-drive off-roader had come round the corner and gone a bit wide.

Hitting him had apparently been inevitable. The problem arose not so much from that as from the fact that the front of the vehicle was decorated with bull bars, and the man's arm had been caught in the bars and almost wrenched off. In addition, he'd fallen, not unnaturally, and one wheel had run over his leg, tearing his arm free from the bars and damaging it almost beyond repair.

He was admitted with serious leg and arm injuries, minor head injuries and severe loss of blood, and their first priority was to stabilise him and notify Theatre that he was coming up for emergency surgery on the arm to restore the circulation before it was too late.

If it wasn't already. She and Ryan were working side by side, and their first task was to get some blood back into him. The artery down his arm was clearly torn in two, and the arm was dangling uselessly. His shoulder joint had been torn apart, the elbow similarly distracted and the humerus between the two was smashed to bits. His forearm was simply broken in the centre, although it was horribly deformed. The leg was broken below the knee, with extensive soft-tissue damage. As the nurse cut away his clothes the tyre tread pattern was revealed, traversing the mangled limb.

Luckily the accident had happened very close to the hospital and so they were able to get onto the situation within a very short time of the injuries taking place, which gave the man a greatly increased chance of not losing either the arm or the leg.

Provided they could stabilise him quickly.

'Portable X-rays,' Ryan snapped to the nurse, who was now hovering for his instructions. 'Now—and four units of O neg, and order ten of cross-matched ASAP. Let's have the blood first.'

Ginny was busy putting on an oxygen mask to give him one hundred per cent oxygen, and as soon as Ryan had finished putting in the large-bore IV line in the man's undamaged right arm and set up the first bag of blood, he handed it over to Ginny.

'Squeeze that into him, fast,' he instructed. A nurse was standing opposite her, carefully trimming cloth away from the damaged arm, and another was beside her—slapping cardiac monitor pads on his chest and linking him up.

The irregular, rapid beep-beep-beep filled the room, all of them unconsciously tuning in to it and listening for any change which might signify deterioration.

Ryan was busy on the undamaged ankle, installing another IV line, and the X-ray machine arrived and took pictures.

'If he lives he'll want them for Court,' Ryan said tersely. 'I'll lay odds the driver hit him at under fifteen miles an hour. Those bull bars are lethal. He was lucky to survive.'

'If he does,' Ginny muttered. She could see the speed at which the blood was flowing out of the mangled arm in her field of vision, despite the nurse's best efforts to stem it, and she thought that the sooner he was in Theatre, frankly, the better.

'We aren't going to get him any better till they sort that out,' Ryan said, following her line of sight. 'Where the

hell—oh, there you are. Zach, this is bad news. You'll
need at least two of you.'

Zach gave a low whistle. 'I'll contact Robert—he's in
his clinic. He'll just have to come out and they'll have to
wait or be rescheduled. This guy won't keep.'

He picked up the phone on the wall, spoke to the head
of his firm and hung up. 'He's on his way. Can I see the
films?'

'Up there.' Ryan jerked his head towards the light box
on the wall.

'Hell's teeth,' Zach muttered. 'Right, I'll take these. Can
you send him up in five minutes? I'll go and scrub.'

He went off at the double, and Ryan and Ginny continued bagging in the blood as fast as possible. The patient's
heart trace was erratic but stable, and his blood pressure
had scraped itself off the floor by the time they transferred
him to Theatre.

'Oh, well, what more can we do?' Ryan said to her as
they scrubbed themselves off. 'We're not God. At least
we've kept him going so they can get at him. It's all down
to them now.'

'Yes—and good luck to them. I don't fancy their job at
all at the moment.'

They heard the following day that the surgical team had
managed to save both arm and badly injured leg, and although things looked grim for the arm it was hoped to
salvage enough function to make the limb useful in a basic
way. The leg was less tricky and would hopefully make a
good recovery, Zach told them.

'So it was all worth it,' Ryan said with a wry grin. 'He'll
live to sue the idiot who hit him. How gratifying.'

'I gather his dog was all right. He'll be pleased about
that. Oh, talking about pets, it's Mabel Walsh's funeral
tomorrow. Can I have an hour off to go?'

'Ooh, now, I don't know about that. I might have to fine you,' he said with a twinkle.

Ginny grinned. 'Yippee,' she said softly.

She phoned her mother that evening before Ryan arrived.

'Hello, darling,' her mother said chattily. 'How are things?'

'Oh, fine. Um—can I bring Ryan and the kids over at the weekend?'

There was a few seconds' silence. 'Of course,' her mother said eventually, much more caution in her voice now. 'When did you have in mind?'

'Saturday or Sunday? Whatever suits you, really.'

'Sunday lunch?'

Ginny could hear the cogs turning. 'Sunday lunch would be fine,' she agreed. 'Oh, and Mum? Don't go and get overexcited about this. Ryan's just a lover, OK? No romantic plans, no future, no wedding bells. This is strictly just an affair, so tell Dad to lay off with the ''What are your prospects, son?'' questions. OK?'

'Darling, you know he wouldn't,' she said, and sounded hurt.

'I just want to be sure. It's difficult enough feeling the way I do about him, without him being pressured by Dad. What time do you want us over?'

'Twelve? What do the children eat?'

'Go for chicken,' Ginny advised her. 'It's safest.'

She told Ryan when he arrived.

'Fine,' he said, and got down to the serious business of kissing her.

Mabel's funeral was small, quiet and rather sad. There were altogether too few mourners, and Ginny was really glad that she'd made the effort to go. There was no gathering afterwards, just a few people standing outside the crematorium, sharing memories. Dora from next door was there, and after a few pleasantries she asked after the cat.

'Oh, he's fine. He's made himself right at home.'

'Good,' Dora said warmly. 'I'd have him myself, but my granddaughter gets asthma and I can't have an animal in the house. He can be quite difficult to keep out in the summer, too.'

Ginny laughed. 'Tell me about it. He's an expert at sneaking through little cracks. I think he could get through a keyhole.'

Dora put her hand on Ginny's arm. 'I'm glad you came, dear. There were never many people who came and visited her—fewer and fewer over the years. That's what happens, I suppose, if you never marry and live to a great age. All your friends and relatives die off before you. Still, at least she was independent right to the end. It could have been a lot worse—and she knew the cat was going to be looked after. That worried her, you know. She loved it when you brought him in.'

'I thought she would. He liked it too. Anything for a bit of love.'

'That's Geronimo all right. Terrible cupboard-lover. My husband was like that!'

They shared a chuckle, and then Dora leant over and said confidingly, 'Saw you with your young man the other evening. My, he's a handsome young devil! I should think he's a bit of a handful! Wherever did you find him?'

Ginny chuckled. 'I work with him.'

'How very distracting,' Dora said with a laugh.

'It is—absolutely—and now, if you'll excuse me, I have to go back and be distracted a bit more!'

She told Ryan what Dora had said, and he actually coloured slightly. 'Do I distract you?' he asked seriously.

'No, of course not. Not when we're really working. There's too much to think about.'

'I'm glad about that. I wouldn't want to be responsible for you not doing things right because I had.'

'The arrogance,' she said, softening her words with a smile. 'As if you could.'

His grin was wicked. 'Want to give it a whirl?'

'Behave,' she told him repressively. 'Start practising for my mother.'

'I shall be the very model of circumspection,' he said primly, and left her to get on in peace, without any further distractions.

Ryan thought Virginia's parents were delightful. Evie and Gus took to them both instantly, and although—unlike Ann's parents—they weren't used to having little children around they didn't spoil them or overindulge them or patronise them.

Ron, her father, took the children off down the garden to study the fish in the pond—and coincidentally give them a safety lecture—while Adele peeled carrots and her daughter basted the roast potatoes, and Ryan was allowed to sit at the table in the kitchen and sip a glass of wine.

'Men aren't designed for cooking—they're designed for entertaining,' Adele said, and refused to let him be useful. 'Talk to us,' she commanded. 'Tell us about Canada.'

So he told them about the wide open spaces and the huge mountains and the stunning colour in the fall, and how the cities were still pleasant places to be, and how cold it was in the winter and how warm in the summer, and that his brother was with the Royal Canadian Mounted Police—and then lunch was ready and they were calling Ron and the children in from the garden.

'Daddy, they've got *huge* fish in the pond,' Angus said,

his eyes like shiny saucers. 'Can we have a pond, please, Daddy?'

'Just a little one?' Evie said.

Virginia hid a smile, and Ryan had to do the same. Already his small daughter was learning the art of nego- tiation, minimising the impact of her demands in order to get her own way more easily.

Ryan wasn't fooled. 'We'll see,' he said.

'That means no,' Evie said pragmatically. 'He always says "we'll see" when he means no but can't say so be- cause he doesn't want to make a scene.'

The adults all but choked at this deadpan delivery of such a pearl of wisdom. Ryan opened his mouth to reason with her, but she just smiled. 'It's true, Daddy,' she said with delightful honesty. 'You know it is.'

'Only sometimes,' he compromised, wondering what on earth else she was going to come up with before the end of lunch.

However, she was the model of decorum from then on, and so was Gus, delighting his hostess with his healthy appetite and well-drilled table manners. Ryan was proud of them. Yes, he thought, they're good kids. The best.

He caught Virginia's eye and winked, and she smiled back, and her warmth filled him. Lord, he thought, we're like a real family. Could it be?

When the meal was over he engineered an opportunity to talk to Ron.

'I wonder, sir, if you'd show me this pond and tell me all about it?' he began. 'If the children want one so badly, perhaps now they're a little older we could consider it. Did you dig it yourself?'

Ron Jeffries laughed and clapped Ryan on the shoulder. 'Heavens, no. Actually it was already here when we moved in. I tell you what, why don't we take a cup of tea down the garden and go and sit by it, and I can explain all the ins and outs?'

Ryan saw Virginia give her mother a panic-stricken look, and smiled reassuringly at her. It didn't seem to work.

'Don't be long,' she told them. 'We can all go for a walk together in a minute.'

It was almost as if she didn't want them together, he thought, and wondered why. Would Ron blurt out the secret Virginia had guarded so faithfully? He hoped not. He wanted her to tell him herself, but that would come with time and trust, and they couldn't be hurried.

They sipped their tea and studied the fish, and then in a little lull Ryan turned to his host and gave him a tentative smile.

'There was another reason for dragging you down here, sir,' he began. 'I wanted to talk to you about Virginia and our relationship. I know it's old fashioned and so on, but that's just the way she makes me feel.'

'I wouldn't have called what she makes you feel old fashioned,' Ron said drily in reply. 'As old as time, maybe. I've seen the way you look at her. She's a pretty girl, I know that, and I can see her feminine attractions. I know you can too, son, so let's not pretend your feelings for her are merely old-fashioned courtship.'

Ryan coloured slightly, but a wry smile touched his lips. 'I never said they were. She lights a fire under me like no woman ever has before, but that's not what I'm talking about. I love her, too, and so do my children, and watching her with them I've realised how lucky we all would be to have her as part of our family. She's got something special—she'll make the perfect wife and mother, and I'm fast reaching the point where I'm going to ask her to marry me and be the mother of my children. I just hope to God she does me the honour of accepting.'

He met Ron's eye unhesitatingly. 'I just wanted to know I had your blessing on that.'

'Oh, but that's wonderful, my boy. Wonderful!' His hand clapped Ryan on the shoulder, squeezing it warmly. 'Oh, you have no idea how good that sounds. D'you know, Adele and I had given up hope of ever having grandchildren. Well, there's only Virginia, and after all this time on her own we wondered if she'd ever settle down. She's been a bit wild, in a way, with one unsuitable man after another while her mother and I worried ourselves sick while she tried to work this thing out of her system, but that's understandable after what happened.

'Terrible, really, but now it won't matter because she'll have your children, and so will we, and I can assure you, Ryan, they'll be loved every bit as much as if they were our own. Oh, Adele will be delighted.'

He leant over confidingly towards Ryan. 'You know, when Virginia had that accident and they told us she'd never have children I thought Adele would never get over it. I mean, seventeen years old and your future wiped out like that. Tragic, it was. Just tragic, and such a stupid thing to happen.'

Ryan's blood ran cold. Accident? he thought. Never have children? Was that the secret?

And he knew, without doubt, that it was.

CHAPTER NINE

GINNY couldn't stand it any longer. She could see her father running off at the mouth, and Ryan getting more and more serious. What on earth was he saying?

'Mum, you promised you'd talk to him,' she said in an undertone, watching nervously from the sitting room window. 'He'll get a shotgun out in a minute—look at Ryan's face!'

Her mother looked down the garden at the two men, then back to the children playing on the rug by the fireplace with their new toys. 'I did talk to him. He promised he'd say nothing. Don't worry, they're probably talking about something totally different.' She glanced back at Ginny, her eyes searching. 'Why do you always refer to him as Ryan and call him O'Connor?' she asked quietly. 'Is it so you can keep an emotional distance?'

Ginny might have known that her mother would see through her so clearly. She jumped up. 'I'm going to get them. I can't stand this. We'll go for that walk.'

She opened the patio doors and went down the garden towards them. Lord, what had he said? Ryan had a face like thunder, and her father was looking disgustingly pleased with himself. That was a bad sign. She took her father by the arm and pulled him to his feet, shooting Ryan a searching look as she did so.

'Come on,' she said, forcing a bright smile. 'We're going for that walk before you frighten Ryan off. Up you get, O'Connor.'

Ryan stood up stiffly. He wasn't looking her in the eye,

but focussing just over her head, and his mouth was a grim line. 'Virginia, I'm sorry to cut the day short but I'm afraid we're going to have to go,' he said, his voice tight. 'My head's playing up—I think I may be going down with something.'

He couldn't look at her. Oh, Lord. He was angry about something—too angry to meet her eyes. She'd find out later what this was about, she had no doubt, but not now, in public. No, he'd get her alone later, she realised, and she was beginning to dread it.

Ron eyed him in concern as they gathered on the drive a few minutes later. 'Will you be all right? Perhaps Virginia ought to drive you.'

'I'll be fine,' he said, and perhaps he only sounded short to Ginny. 'Thank you both so much for a wonderful meal. We've all enjoyed it very much, haven't we, children?'

'Yes, we have,' Evie piped up. 'Thank you so much for the doll.'

'And the fire engine,' Angus added. 'And my lunch. It was lovely. I'm really full!'

They all laughed—all except Ryan. He struggled to produce a weak smile, but got away with it because he was supposedly ill.

Ginny felt ill. Her head was pounding, her blood pressure must be off the scale and she was cold with dread.

Whatever had her father said?

She wasn't destined to find out as soon as she might like. Ryan dropped her off at home with hardly a word, and for the rest of the day she waited for the phone to ring or for him to turn up.

It wasn't until eight-thirty that evening that he arrived to put her out of her misery, by which time she was nearly going crazy.

He must have leant on the doorbell. The sudden shrill

in the silence of her flat was almost the last straw. She opened the door, smoothing her hands nervously on the front of her sweatshirt.

'I expected you earlier,' she told him. She couldn't dredge up a smile, but it would have been wasted anyway. If she'd thought he was angry before, it wasn't a patch on his mood now. He'd obviously spent the intervening period working himself up into a real fury. He strode past her into the kitchen, turned and started almost before the door was closed.

'I had a very interesting conversation with your father earlier,' he began tightly.

She groaned inwardly. Oh, yes, Daddy darling had definitely opened his mouth and put his foot firmly in it, she thought miserably. What had he said?

Ryan didn't bother to explain. He just started in the middle of his train of thought, the leash on his temper snapping as he began to speak.

'Why didn't you tell me?' he demanded icily. 'Why leave it to your father to blurt it out in an inadvertent moment? Nice man, your father, but he's a garrulous old fool. No wonder you were worried about us going down the garden for a little chat. I should think your heart was going nineteen to the dozen in case he dumped you in it.'

'Ryan, I don't know what you're talking about,' she began, but he cut her off with a chilling glare.

'Don't you? Well, let me explain. I told your father I loved you, that I wanted to marry you.'

Her heart leapt in her chest, and then crashed back as she registered the past tense. Loved? Oh, dear God, Ryan, no—

'I even told him I thought you'd make the perfect wife and mother,' he said with a bitter laugh. 'He said how wonderful that would be, seeing as he and your mother had given up hope of ever having grandchildren—since your accident,' he concluded with devastating emphasis.

Her blood ran cold, shock draining the colour from her cheeks. Oh, no, she thought. Not that. Not like that, without any warning. Oh, no.

For the first time Ryan's emotions began to show. 'Why didn't you tell me, Virginia?' he blazed 'Why keep it a secret all this time? What was the big idea?'

'No big idea,' she said hoarsely. 'It wasn't relevant to us—'

'Not relevant? Not *relevant?* How can you say that? I loved you. I wanted to marry you, and all that time you had this huge, burning secret eating you up inside. No wonder you looked so guilty and wretched. The weight of your deceit must have been killing you.'

'Deceit?' she whispered. 'I never lied to you—'

'You didn't confide in me, either. Damn it, Virginia, you kept it secret for weeks, for all the weeks that I was fool enough to fall in love with you—and why? I thought you loved me. I thought you wanted to be part of my family. Instead I realise you wanted to *have* my family. You don't really give a damn about any of us. It was all an elaborate plot to wangle your way into my affections, to gain the children's love and trust, and then close the net around us—your ready-made family. Like buying a TV dinner and bunging it in the microwave. Well, let me tell you something, lady. You can't do that with my family!'

Horror clawed at her throat. 'Ryan, no, it wasn't like that—'

'Ryan now, is it? What's the matter, Virginia, getting desperate? Tell me, did it kill you to pretend to be so interested in me, just to get the kids? Were there any lengths you weren't prepared to go to?'

'But it wasn't like that—'

'Don't lie to me!' he roared. 'I've had it with lies, Virginia! You were using me—using my kids! Damn you, what the hell did you think you were doing? You made us all love you—one after the other we all fell for your scheming lies. And still you didn't tell me! Damn it, I thought you loved me too. I thought there was some meaning to everything we had together, but I was deluding myself, wasn't I? It was just the kids.'

'No, Ryan, you're wrong,' she cried, but he cut her off, his eyes slashing her like lasers.

'I don't think so. Is that why you chose me, out of all the hundreds of unsuitable lovers you've tortured your poor parents with over the years? I should have been warned when you fell into bed with me so willingly that first night. No nice girl would have done that, but I was ready to excuse you—and myself—because I thought we had something really powerful there between us.'

His laugh was brittle. 'And we did, of course. We had your ghastly ambition, didn't we? You should have told me right at the beginning but, no, it would have interfered with your game plan, wouldn't it? Right from the very first moment you had your eyes on me, and I fell for it, hook, line and sinker.' He gave a snort of derision.

'What a gullible fool. You really saw me coming, didn't you? Lonely, sex-starved widower, two sad little children in need of a mother—God, we were sitting ducks! And to think we nearly fell for it! Category Three, my aunt Fanny. You had every intention of being a major player in our lives from the moment you met us. Well, tough, Virginia. You've been rumbled. You're a liar and a cheat and a fraud, and I'm through with you. Thank God you'll never be a mother. You don't have what it takes!'

And with that he pushed past her, wrenched the door open and strode out into the street.

Ginny couldn't move. For now she was numb, shock holding her rigid, but she knew that the pain would come. It had before, swamping her, ripping her apart with its vicious claws, but nothing like this.

Oh, no. She knew instinctively that this time it would be unimaginably worse.

Her legs moving automatically, stiffly, like a robot's, she walked up the hall to the door and very gently closed it, then went back to her own little front door and closed that, too.

Then she rested her head against the panelling and shut her eyes and waited for the pain to come.

It didn't take long. Slowly, insidiously, she felt the tentacles creep around her heart and squeeze—until her breath was gone and she gasped with the agonising pain. Her legs buckled and she turned her back to the door, sliding down until she was sitting on the floor with her legs stuck out, her head back against the panelling, eyes wide and staring.

'It wasn't like that,' she wanted to scream, but her throat wouldn't work. Instead it came out as a dry, harsh scrape, like sandpaper over her nerve-endings. 'It wasn't like that…'

She dragged her legs up, wrapping her arms around her shins and hugging them in to cradle the pain. She rested her head on her knees, his words still lashing round her— the cruel truth of them stripping her to the bone.

She had wanted him from the first moment she saw him. Wanted him and reached out for what she wanted, shamelessly taking what he offered without a second thought. He was right. A nice girl would never have behaved like that, but maybe a nice girl wouldn't have had to face what she had had to face.

No, she couldn't justify it. She had been shameless— but what had he meant about hundreds of lovers? What on earth had her father said to give him that impression? Ryan had implied that she'd tortured her parents with a succession of unsuitable men, but that simply wasn't true. Was he just being cruel? Turning the knife?

No. She knew he wasn't like that. He was hurt, desperately hurt, and he was right that she should have told him, and she would have done had she realised where their relationship was headed, but he wouldn't hurt her unfairly.

Even hurting as she did, she knew the truth of that.

She wished now that she'd told him, but she couldn't turn the clock back. If wishes were horses, she thought, but it was too late now. If she'd told him, he wouldn't have behaved like Simon. Ryan was generous and kind and compassionate, and he wouldn't have discarded her just because she couldn't bear his children. He was too much of a man, too caring, too loyal, but he was still a man, and she wasn't enough of a woman to keep him for ever. Eventually their love would have withered and died under the strain, so perhaps it was just as well. Oh, Ryan...

But it was so hard to be judged so unfairly. How could she make him understand? How could she undo the damage her silence had caused?

And then she knew that she couldn't. He would never understand, never listen to her; never give her a chance to undo the damage she had done.

She had lost him, as she'd always known she would, and the gulf between them would be too wide to bridge.

The cat came and rubbed against her legs, purring and miaowing and nagging for his supper. She stood up stiffly and went to the kitchen, feeding him without thought. The pain was still there, but at least she could stand now.

More or less.

The phone rang. It was her father, calling to find out if Ryan was all right.

'Not really,' she said flatly. 'What on earth did you say to him?'

'What do you mean?' He sounded confused, as if he had no idea what she was talking about. He probably didn't, she thought hollowly.

'About me,' she enlarged. 'What did you say to him about me? Particularly, what did you say about the accident?'

'The accident? Only how upset we both were, and how I thought your mother would never get over it. Nothing more.'

'And how about the hundreds of unsuitable lovers I'm supposed to have tortured you with?'

'What hundreds of lovers?' he said, genuinely puzzled. 'I said you'd gone off the rails a bit—'

'And he misunderstood. I wonder why?' she said bitterly. 'How could you, Dad?' she railed. 'How could you? There were two, Dad. That's all. Two—and you met them both. So why did he think there'd been a whole string?'

'I have no idea—'

'I have,' she snapped, past caring if she upset him. 'You just love to dress things up for impact, and you have no concept of the damage your words do!'

'What damage—?'

'He thinks I'm a whore! He thinks I went after him for the kids. He didn't know the accident had left me unable to have children. He didn't know I love him. He hadn't told me he loved me and wanted to marry me—if he had I would have told him about it, but I didn't think that was what he wanted. I thought he just wanted my body, because that's all I had to give him, and now because of you there's no chance to explain, no chance to let him make the choice, because he's gone and I'll never have another chance—'

She slammed the phone down and then pulled the wire out of the wall. She didn't want any more calls—not from anyone.

Geronimo was waiting on the bed for her, and she undressed and lay down. She was cold inside, so cold. There was nothing left. All Ryan's warmth was gone, and she was alone again.

Except for the cat. She crawled under the quilt and lay there, staring at the pale glow of the ceiling in the light from the streetlamps.

'I love you,' she whispered into the night. 'It wasn't like that. You should have let me explain.' There was a soft squawk, and Geronimo settled heavily down by her chest. She turned and wrapped her arm round him, a huge sob rising in her throat, and the cat squirmed out of her grasp and fled in disgust, leaving her alone again.

Totally, utterly alone…

She walked into the department the following morning, on time and with her loins girded by resolve.

Patrick took one look at her and raised an eyebrow sky-high. 'What the hell happened to you?' he murmured incredulously, searching her face and her body with astonished eyes.

'It's my "sod-you" outfit,' she told him.

He blinked and scanned the short, tight skirt with the kick-pleat, the jumper that lovingly outlined her ample and entirely natural bust, the high heels—topped off by the face paint that she so rarely wore. 'Aimed at?' he asked.

'Need you ask?'

'Actually, no. He's been in his office since eight, crunching pencils. I wondered what was up.' His voice softened. 'Ginny, are you OK?'

She swallowed hard. 'I will be. For God's sake, don't be nice to me.'

He grinned. 'In that case, there's a nasty dose of genital herpes in the first cubicle. Help yourself—oh, and I should do your coat up or you may be examining rather more than you bargained for!'

It was a grim and ghastly morning. Only Patrick, with his comforting wink and understanding grin, kept her going. He took her under his wing at lunchtime and marched her over the road to the pub for a quick lunch, ran interference for her with Ryan when a patient demanded to see the senior doctor on duty and Jack was missing, and generally kept an eye on her.

Unfortunately there was something he couldn't do for her, and that was face Ryan and hand in her notice.

She tracked him down in his office late in the afternoon—in a welter of bits of wood and broken pencil leads.

He glared at her. 'What the hell do you think you've got on? You can't work dressed like that, it's inappropriate.'

'So sack me, O'Connor.'

His mouth tightened. 'Don't tempt me. What do you want?'

'To give you this.'

She passed the handwritten letter to him, dropping it on the pile of shattered pencils. He slit the envelope, yanked out the letter and scanned it. 'Fine. Accepted. Was there anything else?'

Her heart was shattering, destroyed just like the pencils that littered his desk.

'No—not that you'd listen to,' she said quietly. 'I'll work my notice because I have to, but if you could manage to engineer it so we don't have to spend time together I think it would be a good idea.'

He looked right through her. 'Don't worry. I've already rewritten the schedule. You're with Patrick from now on. Just remember one thing.'

She waited, one brow raised a fraction, her face carefully schooled.

'He's a happily married man. Leave him alone.'

She stifled the gasp, but he must have heard the tiny indrawn breath.

'You're despicable,' she said softly, and turned and walked out. Just before she shut the door she heard another pencil bite the dust. Good. Damn him. That was it—stay angry. It took the hurt away, drowned it out—

'Ginny?'

She stopped, her head close to a broad, inviting chest. 'Oh, Patrick,' she sighed, and she felt her eyes filling. She scrubbed them with a tissue, but they filled again and overflowed, taking great streaks of mascara down her cheeks.

She felt his arm around her shoulders, his body solid against her side like a rock in the wild, restless sea, and she rolled her face into his chest and bit her lip. The sob wasn't stopping, though, nor the next one. Her feet worked mechanically, one in front of the other, and Patrick guided her into a room and shut the door.

Then he pushed her into a chair, took the one beside her and put his arm round her again. 'That's right,' he murmured comfortingly, 'get it off your chest.'

She did—and all over his. When she finally lifted her head his shirt was covered in mascara and he looked a wreck. What she looked like, she neither dared to consider nor cared. 'I've ruined your shirt,' she sniffed.

'That's all right. I've got a very understanding wife.'

'Ryan warned me off you,' she said woodenly. 'He said you were happily married and I was to leave you alone.'

Patrick's mouth tightened into a grim line. 'What the

hell happened between you two to cause World War Three?'

She sighed and closed her eyes. 'It's a long story.'

'So tell me.'

She shook her head. 'Not here. Not now. I'll fold up again and I can't work when I'm howling my eyes out. I tend to go blind.'

'Go home,' he told her. 'It's nearly five. I'll finish off, give Anna a ring and pop round.'

'There's no need—' she began, but he just smiled.

'Oh, yes, there is,' he said softly. 'Go on. Have a quick wash first, go home and put the kettle on then you can tell Uncle Patrick all about it.'

She did as he said, mainly because she didn't have any stuffing left to argue with. Geronimo was outside when she arrived, waiting for her in a patch of early autumn sunshine on the bench by the kitchen window. She opened the door, put the kettle on and went and changed into jeans and a ragged sweatshirt, before stripping the streaked remains of her make-up from her washed-out skin.

The doorbell rang and she went and let Patrick in. He followed her down to the kitchen and watched her as she poured boiling water on the teabags. 'I feel so silly,' she began, and then the tears welled up again and she put the kettle down with a little thump and sagged over the worktop.

Lord, that pain would keep getting her just when she was least expecting it! There was no warning. It had been happening all day. One minute she'd be fine, the next something he'd said would spring into her mind and she'd crumple up like a soggy tissue.

Patrick led her outside, sat her down next to the cat and went in again, reappearing a few moments later with two cups of tea.

'Here,' he told her. 'Take that and don't burn yourself.'

She scrubbed her eyes on her hands and took the cup, then sighed. 'Sorry. It just gets me.'

Patrick left her alone for a moment to pull herself together, then stretched out his long legs, rested his cup on his belt buckle in his usual attitude and glanced across at her. 'OK,' he said, 'tell Uncle Patrick.'

She took a nice, deep, steadying breath. 'You remember that accident I told you about?'

'When you were a teenager?'

She nodded. 'Remember I had internal injuries? When they opened me up they found they needed the gynae team as well.'

'Oh, bloody hell. I don't think I want to hear this.'

'They did a hysterectomy. One of my ovaries was smashed and the other one was useless anyway, apparently, so there wasn't a lot of point in trying to rescue what was left of my uterus, so they didn't. They took it all out, tidied me up and did the best job they could with the scars. So now I look like a real woman, but it's all just a hollow sham.'

Her voice was flat and dead. This bit of the story she could deal with. It was the bit with Ryan in that killed her every time she allowed her mind to linger on it.

Patrick was silent for a long time, then he put his tea down, sat forwards and propped his elbows on his knees and stared at the ground between his feet. 'So what happened with Ryan?' he asked carefully.

'Oh—he found out yesterday. My father dropped the bombshell. Anyway, it's all over now.'

Patrick stared at her. 'Why?'

She shook her head. 'I'm sorry, I can't talk about it.' The pain welled up again, but she squashed it.

'He dumped you because of that?'

'It wasn't exactly a surprise,' she told him. 'Well, not once he found out that I couldn't give him children. It's what a man wants, isn't it?'

'Is it?' he asked softly.

'Yes, of course it is. It always has been, since the beginning of time.'

'That's not why I wanted Anna—or Isobel. Isobel had spina bifida. There was no question of her having children, but I married her anyway. I loved her.'

Ginny swallowed hard. 'Then she was a very fortunate woman.'

His hand covered hers, hard and strong. 'Ginny, Ryan has kids, anyway. It couldn't be better. I don't see the problem.'

'Don't you?' she said bleakly. 'I didn't tell him, that was the problem. I didn't think it was necessary, not for the kind of relationship we had. Anyway, I was rather enjoying him telling me I was all woman. I was able to pretend for a while.' She looked down at his hand and placed her other one over it, for comfort. 'Then my father dropped the bombshell, and Ryan went berserk. He thinks I wanted him just for the kids.'

'That's stupid. Anyone can see you love him.'

'Ryan can't.'

'Then he's a fool,' Patrick growled. His hand tensed between hers, and she smoothed the taut skin and idly traced the pattern of veins on the back.

'No. He's hurt. Anyway, I'm leaving.'

'What?'

He snatched his hand back and turned to face her. 'What?' he repeated more loudly.

She shrugged. 'I have to. I can't stay; surely you can see that.'

'Ginny, you have to stay and sort this out with Ryan.'

She shook her head sadly. 'No. There's nothing to sort out. It's over, Patrick. I just have to let it go.'

He was appalled. 'You're crazy! How about your future? What about your career, if nothing else?'

She met his eyes, her own empty. 'What *about* my career, Patrick? Just now I couldn't give a stuff about my career. I just want to get away.' She looked back at her hands. 'He's put us together on the schedule, so he doesn't have to work with me. I hope that won't make trouble with Anna.'

'Why should it? She trusts me.'

'Aren't you lucky?' Ginny said quietly. 'How very, very fortunate.'

'I am,' he agreed. 'Ginny, I'm sorry. I wish there was something I could do.'

'There is. You can keep him away from me, and hold my hand for the next month until I can escape.' She gave him a shaky smile. 'You're a love, Patrick. Thanks for everything.'

He stood up, bent and kissed her cheek, and took their mugs into the kitchen. 'Get some rest,' he advised, slouching in the doorway, 'and by the way, for what it's worth you look better dressed like that.'

She smiled. 'I know. It doesn't annoy him as much, though.'

Patrick chuckled and shook his head. 'I'm going. See you in the morning—and if you need anything, just shout.'

'Thanks.'

She watched him go, then slowly stood up and went in. She tidied up, did some ironing, cleaned the kitchen—

'Busy work,' she mocked herself, but it passed the time and kept her mind in neutral.

Frankly, it was the best place to be.

*   *   *

The next few days were hell. Ryan looked terrible, and she supposed that she did too. She gave up with the defiant dressing and concentrated on keeping out of his way. Any words they exchanged were minimal, and any time they had to spend together was a nightmare.

The only conversation she instigated in that first week he cut off with deliberate cruelty, until she wasn't sure if she had ever known him at all.

He was in the staffroom when she went in to get a cup of coffee. She could have turned and walked out, but she wanted a drink and she didn't see why she should go without.

He stood there and watched her, his face blank and carefully expressionless but his eyes burning like hot coals. He was drinking her in, which was silly because she'd abandoned the sexy gear in favour of a plain silk mix jumper and a very demure knee-length skirt. Still, his eyes followed her every move, and she felt distinctly uncomfortable.

She made conversation just for the sake of breaking the awful silence.

'How are the children?' she asked quietly.

There was a deathly hush. 'Confused, hurt—what do you expect? I told them you didn't want to see us any more.'

'But that's a lie!' she exclaimed, shocked and saddened that he could do that to his children.

'Yes, I know—but better than the truth, I think. I could hardly tell them that they were just a commodity, could I? That I was, too, just a means to an end? All that hot sex and endless enthusiasm—how much of it was faked, Virginia? All those breathless little climaxes—perhaps I should nominate you for an Oscar?'

She dropped the cup from nerveless fingers and, whirling on the spot, she ran for the door—smack into Patrick's iron-hard chest.

He caught her, steadied her and let her go, then a few minutes later he came and found her.

'Have a look at my lip, could you?' he muttered.

She scrubbed the tears off her cheeks and turned, and her eyes widened. 'Oh, Patrick, what the hell have you been up to?'

'I ran into a door,' he said mildly.

'More like a fist. Why are you fighting over me? Anna will get worried.'

'Rubbish. I'll tell her a patient did it.'

'No!' she exclaimed, horrified. 'Tell her the truth, or I will.'

'You don't know the truth,' he reminded her.

She dabbed at his lip with a piece of gauze soaked in saline. 'What a mess. Anyway, I do. You got all protective.'

'He can't talk to you like that,' Patrick said quietly. 'Not in a public place, at least.'

'But brawling! How did he come off?'

Patrick snorted. 'You care?'

Damn it, yes, she did care. 'Did you leave a bruise?'

'I damn well hope so. My knuckles hurt like hell.'

She examined his hand, and tutted. 'You've been lucky. You could have broken your metacarpals.'

'Big wow. It would have been worth it.'

She cleaned him up and sent him on his way, then went to find Jack.

'What the hell's going on?' he said shortly. 'You look like death warmed up, Patrick's going round with a split lip and Ryan's got a black eye. Also I gather you've handed in your notice. I'd like to know what's happening.'

'We're all busy proving it's not a good idea to mix

business with pleasure,' she told him calmly. Then, as casually as she could manage, she said, 'Is Ryan all right?'

'He'll live. He's gone into his office with an ice pack. For God's sake stay away from him before someone gets killed.'

So she did. It made life a great deal easier for everyone concerned, and it worked like a charm—right up until the beginning of the following week.

Then all their avoidance tactics were wasted—because they were forced together by circumstances beyond their control. There was a gas explosion in a big old Victorian terrace which contained dozens of bedsits and squats and was peopled by some very dodgy characters.

Half the glass in the street was wiped out, buildings collapsed in heaps of rubble and there were massive numbers of people with injuries of varying severity.

The hospital put its Major Incident Plan into operation immediately, and the first thing Jack Lawrence did was call a meeting of all the A and E staff—from receptionist through to anaesthetists and surgeons who were seconded to the unit at a moment's notice.

'The first thing to do is sort out who's staying and who's going,' he said. 'We need a qualified, experienced team here to handle the casualties as they arrive, and another team out in the field to deal with triage, sorting the casualties into priority order for relay back here, treatment on the spot of any trapped or very seriously injured casualties and so on.

'Ryan, you're Incident Medical Officer—you'll need a team with you of three nurses and a doctor. I can't spare Patrick; I need him here. You'd better take Ginny.' He glared at him. 'And God help you if you can't manage to bury your personal differences for the course of this operation.'

CHAPTER TEN

IT WAS a scene of organised chaos when they arrived. Ginny went with Ryan to meet the Incident Control Officer or ICO, who was a senior police officer. Ryan introduced himself as the IMO and was immediately directed to where the majority of casualties were assembling.

'There are several doctors here looking for jobs,' they were told. 'If you could co-ordinate them?'

Ryan nodded and turned to the waiting doctors. 'We've got all sorts of equipment—coats, record cards and so on—arriving now. I'll get you all equipped with what you need and we can get on. I want all casualties, no matter how slightly injured or how seriously, directed through A and E at the Audley, so whatever you have to do, do it and make sure they know they have to go and be checked out.

'All casualties are to have an emergency number and a set of emergency case notes. There are record cards here—' he held one up '—with a clinic record on one side and a status record on the other. Decide which category they fit from minor, serious, critical or dead, fill in the clinic information and put the card into the plastic sleeve with the category on the outside, and pin it to the casualty. Hopefully we won't get too many of the last category.

'Anyone critical obviously needs urgent attention. I'm going to be doing the triage, going from one to the other of you checking your patients and getting them away as quickly as possible according to need. We'll have facilities here for emergency work, and obviously equipment for putting in intravenous lines, getting drips going with plasma expander and so on. Anyone in any doubt about what they're doing, for God's sake, ask. Right, get your equipment and get to it.'

He turned to Ginny. 'You know what to do. Just keep calm and do your best.'

She nodded, collected her gear and went over to where the casualties were assembling. Ryan was already there, wearing his distinctive coat that identified him from the others, and he was sorting out the worst of the injured.

'Virginia, get a line in this man fast,' he instructed. 'Bag in some Haemaccel, then get him on his way. He's bleeding from internals. Here, I've started a card.'

He flipped her the card and moved on, and she took over. The patient despatched to hospital, she started on the next and then the next, wondering as she did so where they all came from.

Some were cut quite severely by flying glass, others hit by falling masonry, still others just shocked or deafened by the blast.

One man had been driving his car past at the time of the explosion and had been thrown across the road, and had sustained a nasty head wound and broken arm. Others had been thrown to the ground and were grazed and terrified.

Shock was the most common feature, and she reassured and comforted and covered nasty grazes and wondered how on earth they were coping back in A and E.

Jack needn't have worried about her and Ryan, she thought. After the first few minutes she'd hardly seen him. She gathered he'd gone into the building to deal with a trapped casualty, but since then she'd seen nothing of him.

And then, without any warning, there was another massive explosion in the building.

Her head came up, her eyes widened and she stared in

horror as the dust swirled away, leaving the street silent but for the sound of tinkling glass.

A child started to cry, and the sound released Ginny from her trance. 'Ryan?' she whispered and, standing up, she started running towards the crumbling building. 'Ryan? Ryan, where are you?' she screamed.

Oh, dear God, he was in there, his body crushed and mangled, the life being forced out of him by the weight of rubble. She had to find him, had to get him out—

'Ryan!' she screamed again, and started clawing at the lumps of masonry, heaving them aside and searching desperately for a glimpse of that distinctive coat.

Then she heard his voice behind her and turned. 'Virginia!' he yelled. 'What the hell are you doing? Get out of there!'

He was running towards her, his face a mask of terror, and as she registered that he was still alive he reached her—just as there was a dull 'whump' from the building and the world slowly caved in on top of them…

'Virginia?'

She was dreaming. He was saying her name as if she was the most important thing in his world, and it sounded wonderful. She turned towards his voice, coughing in the choking clouds of dust and smoke, and found a cloth held over her mouth. She breathed through it, resisting the urge to push it away, and gradually her mind cleared.

'Ryan?' she whispered.

'Oh, thank God,' he muttered raggedly, and she thought, How odd, he sounds really stressed. Almost as if he cares. Maybe I am dreaming.

And then she felt the pain. Her eyes closed, and a funny whimpering sound seemed to leak out of her chest.

'Virginia?' he was saying. 'Where do you hurt?'

'My legs,' she said as calmly as she could because she'd just discovered that she couldn't move them and she was trapped. 'I think I'm stuck here for a bit.'

He swore, softly but comprehensively, and then she could feel his hand working its way down her body, feeling for injuries. He stopped just below her knees, and swore again. 'Can you move your toes?' he asked.

She tried. 'No. I would be able to, but my feet are stuck under a lump of something rather heavy. I can feel the muscles contracting, though.'

She thought she felt him relax a little, but not much. 'Are you in a lot of pain?' he asked next.

'A fair bit,' she told him matter-of-factly. 'I've felt worse.'

'Your accident,' he said, and muttered something under his breath. 'Look, I'm going to see if I can find a way out to the outside, OK?'

'OK,' she said as calmly as she could. She wanted to scream, No, don't leave me, but it didn't seem quite British so she shut up and gritted her teeth and tried not to cry.

'I'll come back,' he promised.

'Fine. Bring me an aspirin.'

She saw him turn his head in the dim light that filtered in. 'Was that supposed to be a joke?' he said incredulously.

'Of course not. I'm stuck here under tons of rubble, waiting for the next explosion—why should I crack jokes?' She gave him a push. 'Just get on with it, O'Connor, and don't mess about.'

After a second's hesitation he crawled away from her, but he didn't get far. 'I can see daylight,' he told her over his shoulder, 'and I can hear people shouting for us. I'll call back.' He turned towards the chink of light. 'Hey! In here!' he yelled.

'Doc? Is that you?' The voice was distant and distorted,

but at least it was contact. Ginny made herself breathe regularly and tried not to panic. They'd been pinpointed now. They'd soon have her out of there.

She could hear the shift and scrape of stone, and knew their rescuers were clearing the rubble around their chink of light.

Suddenly the light became much brighter.

'What's happening?' she asked Ryan.

'They're clearing a way through,' he told her. 'Hang on.'

But there was a hitch. A huge girder was in the way, and they could only clear a tunnel wide enough for an arm.

She looked at it despairingly. 'Well, unless they take us out of here in pieces, I reckon we're stuck in here together, whether we like it or not, O'Connor,' she told him drily, and even through her pain she could tell that he wasn't thrilled by the idea of being trapped with her.

'Don't worry, they'll do something soon, then I'll be able to get in and out.'

Especially out. She moved her legs again experimentally, and nearly cried out with the pain. Damn. Not a good move. She turned her head away from him, and found a huge block of masonry just inches from her face. She didn't remember it being there before the explosion. As realisation of her predicament and close call sank in she began to shake with shock and reaction.

Tears clogged her lashes, fear rose like bile in her throat and she retched helplessly.

'Virginia? Oh, hell,' Ryan muttered, and then one arm was round her, his other hand was smoothing her hair back off her face and he was making reassuring noises.

It was wonderfully comforting—or it would have been if it had been Patrick or someone like him who was kind and caring and didn't hate her guts.

She bit down on the sob that threatened. 'Sorry,' she muttered. 'I don't know why I chucked up.'

'Shock, pain—don't worry about it.' He moved away a little and she felt the separation like a physical wrench. 'I'll see if I can get some light and some blankets and things in here so I can make you more comfortable and get a look at your legs.'

He crawled away again, calling through the hole to the rescuers working outside. She must have lost consciousness for a moment because the next thing she was aware of was a bright light being shone in her eyes.

'Ow, that's bright,' she complained, pushing his hand away.

She thought she heard him sigh, but whether with relief or irritation she wasn't sure. Irritation, probably.

'Let me check your pupils,' he said.

'They're fine. Check my legs.'

'Allow me to be the judge of what's fine,' he said caustically. 'Look straight ahead—lovely. And the other one—fine.'

'I said they were.'

'And isn't it nice to be proved right?' he came straight back. 'Now, about these legs.'

He squirmed down towards her feet, and she lifted her head a fraction and looked down where he was pointing the pen-torch. She wished she hadn't. There seemed to be an awful lot of brickwork balanced just over her feet, and it looked mighty precarious.

'Just don't move anything,' she gritted.

'I won't,' he assured her. 'Right, I can see your legs now, and there's a door or something like that across them. It's actually supporting quite a lot of other rubble so it's doing you a favour. The weight on your feet is a lintel of some sort, I think. Whatever, the circulation looks reasonable, but I think your right leg's broken and the left leg definitely is.'

'I noticed,' she said drily. 'Look, the aspirin was a joke but I don't suppose you could knock up some kind of pain relief, could you? A general anaesthetic or something?'

He crawled back up to her face. 'I need to take your blood pressure first and be sure you can tolerate the depressive effect—'

'For heaven's sake, I've got a couple of broken bones not internal injuries! Of course I can tolerate the depressive effect of the drugs! The sooner the better.'

His face was taut. 'Yes, sir,' he muttered and, turning away, he crawled towards the hole. She could hear him yelling instructions again, but she was slipping nicely into oblivion for the second time and didn't really care what he was talking about, just so long as he was getting her something to take away the pain.

Her eyes closed and she turned her head a little, noticing for the first time how uneven and bumpy the ground was that they were lying on.

Of course, it wasn't ground at all, it was rubble. How silly. No wonder it was sticking into her in all directions. She shifted her shoulders a fraction and felt a sharp, stabbing pain in her side. She moved her hand cautiously round under her coat, and felt a warm, sticky mess just above her waist. Wonderful, she thought. A penetrating injury. Terrific.

'O'Connor?'

He crawled back to her side. 'Yes?'

'Something's sticking in me,' she told him.

'Hang on a minute, then, and I'll get you a blanket to cushion your back from the rubble.'

'No. I mean, something's sticking into me. Like, in.'

He went very, very still. 'Where?' he asked softly.

'My left side. Just above my waist.'

His hand slid round over her ribcage and felt carefully around the area, and then he swore under his breath.

'Come again?' she murmured drily.

'It's a nail. It's probably only just under the skin. Can you feel any pain when you move or breathe?'

She resisted the urge to laugh or make a sick joke. It wasn't really very difficult. She only had to remind herself that she was trapped—

'A little,' she told him. 'Nothing drastic.'

He met her eyes. 'I want to get an IV line into your arm—just to be on the safe side. Your legs are losing blood into the tissues with the fractures, and if your side's losing it too you could need some top-up sooner or later. If I've got a line in it'll make it much easier if we have to top you up fast.'

'I do understand the routine,' she told him candidly.

'That's the problem,' he muttered under his breath.

She caught his arm. 'It's no problem, O'Connor. You just do what you have to do and I'll lie here and be the model patient. Just tell them to get their butts into gear and get us out of here, OK?'

Lord, those eyes were lovely and for the first time in ages they weren't looking at her with disgust and derision, but with concern and even respect. They swam out of focus, and she dropped her lids down and let him go.

'Just hurry,' she said with as much calm as she could muster.

He gave her hand a quick squeeze and then he was gone, shouting through the crack again. It seemed like for ever but then finally he was there, and she felt the sharp prick of the cannula going into her arm and then wonderfully, mercifully, the pain slid away.

Well, not really away. She could still feel it, but she

couldn't bring herself to care. She was much too interested in Ryan's hair, just inches from her face. She reached out her other hand and touched it.

It was stiff with dust, and she smoothed it back. 'Thank you,' she murmured. Then she couldn't be bothered to think any more...

Ryan felt sick. When he'd seen the building creak and shift his only thought had been to get her out of the way. There had been no thought for his own safety, for the children he would leave behind if he died. Just his beloved Virginia, with tons of masonry teetering over her head, apparently looking for him in the rubble.

Had she thought he'd been trapped in the blast just before? Maybe so. He could have been; he'd been in the building just moments before, and they'd come out because of the smell of gas. She'd been calling his name when he'd looked up and seen her.

Not O'Connor either, said in that semi-mocking tone of hers, but Ryan—in a voice filled with terror and anguish.

Why?

She didn't really love him, so why sound so anguished?

He checked the IV line and set up the saline, running it in slowly. Her blood pressure was quite good, a little low but not bad, considering. The morphine had taken effect now and her body had relaxed, giving up its fight. He felt round the nail in her side again, and found another a little further along. If they were the same size then this one was only long enough to do superficial damage. He'd risk it and roll her off if she wasn't trapped by her feet, but there was nothing he could do to help her at the moment if its removal would cause any major problems.

He left her there, still impaled, and checked her legs again. The circulation seemed good, both feet reasonably warm under her socks, although her left leg was swelling badly now and needed urgent attention.

She'd get crush syndrome when they released her, he realised. She'd have to go straight to ITU for dialysis, probably, because of the mass of damaged protein cells that would enter her bloodstream and clog her kidneys. Her legs would probably have to wait.

If they got her out.

She turned her head towards him and opened her eyes. 'Ryan?' she whispered. 'Is it really you?'

He took her hand. 'Yes, Virginia, it's me.'

'Are you sure? You haven't been talking to me for ages. Why are you here?'

'We're trapped inside the rubble,' he told her.

'Rubble? Oh, yes, the building. Am I trapped too?'

'Yes, you are. How are your legs?'

'What legs?' she asked, and started to giggle. 'I don't have any legs. They hurt. I don't want them any more. Can I have yours? You've got sexy legs.'

Lord, she was off, he thought. Away with the fairies. 'Just close your eyes and go to sleep,' he told her. Anything but lie there and tell him he'd got sexy legs in that smoky voice of hers.

She went quiet for a while, then she opened her eyes again and looked at him.

'Ryan?' she whispered.

'Yes?'

'I feel weird. Sort of light-headed.'

'I gave you some morphine.'

'Really? Why would anybody want it? I mean, for recreation.'

'God knows,' he muttered.

'I tried cannabis once. I was sick. That was the night of my accident. I don't remember all that much about it.'

'Tell me about the accident,' he asked, hating himself for pumping her when she was out of it and wouldn't remember but still needing to know. 'What happened to you?'

'A bit of bridge went into my ab-adbo—oh, hell. Tummy. I was all messed up inside. Ruptured this and that. They took out all sorts of things.'

'What sorts of things?' he pushed, not really wanting to hear but unable to stop himself from asking.

'My bowel, great chunks of it,' she sang, waving an arm. 'My left kidney—oh, an' my ut'rus. It was shredded up, and my ov'ry was squashed, so they just took it all out.'

Ryan caught her hand before she dislodged the drip. Her fingers locked round his and she sighed. 'Tha's nice,' she mumbled. 'I thought you didn't want me any more.'

Damn his feeble hide, he'd never stopped wanting her. He closed his eyes.

'Ryan?'

He opened them again and found her face turned towards him, those soft grey eyes clouded with pain and confusion fixed on his like a lifeline.

'Yes?'

'I'm cold.'

He pulled a blanket under her shoulders and round over her chest, and eased her into his arms. If only she didn't have that nail in her side it would be much easier, but he daren't move her. She sighed and relaxed her head against his shoulder, and he brought his hand up and smoothed her hair away from her face. It was all stiff with plaster dust, thick and rough, not at all like the wonderfully soft shining curtain it really was.

Still he stroked it, and it seemed to soothe her for a while.

Outside he could hear scraping and digging noises, quite close by, and he hoped as they drew closer they wouldn't do anything too silly to dislodge the precarious ceiling of their prison.

It was good to hold her again, he thought heavily. He'd missed her so much. The pain that never really left him stabbed again with unrelenting fervour, and he tightened his hold fractionally and pressed his lips to her dust-stiff hair. How could he still love her—after all she'd done to him and the children?

'Oh, God, Virginia, why?' he murmured.

She stirred in his arms, her hand coming up to cup his cheek. 'I love you,' she whispered.

He closed his eyes. She sounded drunk. You couldn't pay any attention to the ramblings of a drunk.

'I'm sorry I'm not a real wom'n,' she went on hazily. 'I always felt like one with you, as if it didn't matter that I was just a fraud. All empty inside,' she said mournfully, and then she sobbed a tiny bit, just once or twice.

'I thought you were dead just now,' she went on after a little pause, and this time she sounded more lucid. 'I thought the building had fallen on you, and you'd be dead, smashed to pieces, gone. I wanted to die, too. Please don't die. I love you.'

Her hand on his cheek was fluttering, tentative and almost afraid to believe he was there. He took it in his and held it between them, against his heart. 'I won't die,' he assured her.

'Promise?' she whispered.

Lord, how foolish. There were tons of rubble up above them, just waiting for another explosion or an unwary move to come tumbling down on their heads. 'I promise,' he said rashly.

That seemed to satisfy her for a while, but then she

started again. 'It wasn't like that, you know,' she said. 'I never thought you'd want me—only my body. I didn't mean to fall in love with you. That was so, so silly, wasn't it? 'Specially when you hate me.'

He groaned softly. 'I don't hate you, Virginia. I want to, but I can't. Whatever you've done, why ever you've done it, it seems I love you anyway.'

Lord, he thought, the morphine was getting to him too, acting like some kind of infernal truth drug.

'Ryan?' she murmured.

He opened his eyes again and looked at her. 'Yes, honey?'

'Tell me that again.'

He sighed and gave in to the inevitable. 'I love you,' he confessed.

'We weren't supposed to, were we?' she said, sounding muddled. 'Fall in love, I mean. We were supposed to have an affair—just that. No string. No future. Just an affair.' She eased her hand from his and touched his cheek again. 'It was wonderful, you know, just to pretend I was a real woman. That's why I didn't tell you. It was only an affair—just Category Three. You didn't need to know, so I could pretend and enjoy all that attention that you wouldn't have given me if you'd known.'

She sighed. 'Then we went and spoilt it by falling in love, so you had to find out, and now you hate me. It always happens. Simon hated me when he found out, Rick said I'd cheated him—and now you think it's all for your children. Funny, that. I didn't want to have too much to do with you because I didn't want the kids getting hurt, and you said it was all to get to them. Why, when it was just an affair? I knew you'd never marry me.'

'How did you know that?' Ryan asked, hardly daring to breathe.

'Of course you wouldn't. I'm no good. I know that. No man wants just half a woman. It was just fun to make believe for a while; to play house. It was like being a kid again, except the stakes were real people and it all got a bit too messy, didn't it?' She stroked his cheek. 'I'm sorry. I shouldn't have played games with you, but I couldn't help it. I just wanted you so much, and you were so lonely. I didn't think it could hurt.'

She was quiet for a moment, then said, 'Ryan? My legs hurt. I think this morphine's wearing off.'

She was shaking in his arms, with reaction and with cold, and he eased away and checked her blood pressure again. It was falling, and suddenly he had an almost paralysing fear that she was going to die before he had a chance to talk to her and get her side of the story.

Not now, not while she was under the influence of hallucinogenic drugs, but when she was sober and wide awake and coherent.

Because he had the sudden, terrible feeling that he had been horribly wrong about her, and that she was going to die before he could say he was sorry...

It was two days before Ginny was properly awake and free from drugs, and in that two days Ryan had had some very enlightening chats with Ron Jeffries. He might be a garrulous old fool but he loved his daughter to distraction, and he was furious with Ryan for hurting her so badly.

He was also furious with himself for having given the wrong impression and having caused so much trouble, and he was doing his level best to make amends.

Ryan learned that Ginny's going off the rails had been in a very minor way and more to do with depression than a frenzied search for sex. There had been only two affairs, he learned, both of which she'd mentioned and both of which had ended in disaster.

'The bastards both told her they loved her and then dumped her because she couldn't give them children,' Ron told him as they sat by her bedside on the second day and watched her sleep. 'I think she gave up hope after that. She told Adele she was going to swear off men for life, but then she met you. I'm surprised she entertained the idea of an affair like that—she's always been very wary of casual sex, but maybe she thought it was time to let go and start living a little.

'You know, it was funny watching her with your children,' he went on. 'She's always been good with children, but she's never really been that bothered about them before. Yours, though, she really seems to love. Adele commented on it—said how well they got on and how much she loved them. She's always kept away before because she couldn't have any—to avoid stirring up the hurt, I suppose. She must have really let you all into her heart to spend time with you like that.'

Ryan closed his eyes. He wanted to turn back the clock and have that conversation with her again, without flying off the handle or jumping to endless conclusions. If only he could! He'd said so many terrible, cruelly hurtful things to her. If he'd made a mistake, as he was now almost sure he had, and he'd been wrong about her, then only turning back the clock and taking those words away would heal the pain she must be suffering.

Life, though, wasn't like that. If it was Virginia would have turned back the clock and never gone to that party, he would have turned back the clock and never come up to Suffolk the weekend Ann was killed, Patrick would have turned back the clock and saved Isobel from the earthquake—so many lives would have been different.

No. He couldn't turn back the clock. All he could do was try again—and he'd start with an apology...

Ginny hurt. Her legs hurt, her side hurt but most of all her heart was breaking. Ryan was there. She knew he was. She could hear him—talking softly to her father, sitting at her bedside for hour after hour.

For a short while, in the hazy cocoon of that broken building, she had managed to fool herself that he loved her. Now, in the cold light of day, she realised that she had dreamt it all. She'd been hallucinating, foolish thing that she was, trying to make the things come true that she wanted to be so.

And Ryan loving her was at the top of the list.

So why was he still hanging about here? It must be hours later. She opened her eyes.

'O'Connor?' she croaked.

He stood up and came over to her instantly, and she looked at his beloved face and saw bruises and scrapes and cuts all over it.

'You look a mess,' she told him candidly. 'Don't, for God's sake, give me a mirror to look in.'

He smiled slightly. 'You look wonderful,' he lied.

'Don't lie,' she chastised.

He perched a hip on the edge of the bed and picked up the hand that didn't have a drip in. 'I wasn't. How are you feeling?'

'Just peachy. What time is it?'

'Five-thirty.'

'Is that all? I thought it must be later than that. We didn't get called there till lunchtime, and I thought we were trapped for hours.'

His thumb stroked her hand, making it difficult to concentrate on anything else. 'That was Monday. This is Wednesday.'

'Wednesday!' she exclaimed. 'Wednesday?'

He nodded, and she fell back against the pillows. No wonder she felt so rough. 'How about my legs?' she asked after a moment spent assimilating her time warp.

'They're OK. The left one's pinned. The right one was a nice clean fracture. You've got a cast on them both.'

'You don't say,' she said drily. She could feel the casts—they were as heavy as lead, not to mention sore. She allowed herself to look at him. 'Why are you here?' she asked, dreading the answer and yet wanting to get rid of him so that she could cry her eyes out and feel better.

He wanted to look away. She could tell that, but he didn't allow himself to. His eyes burned like emeralds in his battered face. 'Because I love you. Because we need to talk. Because I owe you an apology, and I'm not sure anything I could say would be enough to make up for what I've done to you.'

She swallowed hard. 'Cut to the chase, O'Connor,' she mocked, unable to believe what she was hearing. 'Apologise for what? Terrifying the lights out of me? Not dying in the explosion? Giving me too much morphine?'

'For saying all the things I said to you,' he told her bleakly. 'After Ann died I thought I'd always be alone. I couldn't believe anyone would want to take on someone else's kids. Then, just when I thought I'd found someone who would, I managed to convince myself that it was the kids who were the draw and not me.'

He looked up at her. 'I thought you hadn't told me because you were keeping it a secret until we were married so I didn't rumble your plan to get your perfect ready-made family. Then you told me you'd said nothing because you wanted to pretend you were a real woman.' He gave a strained little laugh. 'You were up to your eyebrows in morphine, and it was the stupidest thing I'd ever heard. It just had to be true.'

'But it is true,' she said matter-of-factly. 'That's exactly why I didn't tell you. Twice I'd been dumped because I was honest. Men don't want women who aren't real. I just pretended to be real. I didn't think it could hurt. After all, you'd made it clear you only wanted an affair so it couldn't do any harm, but it could, of course, because you went and fell for me, and me for you, and it all went wrong because you fell for a lie and not the real thing.'

'But you are real. That's so crazy. I've never known a woman who was more woman than you.'

Her eyes filled. 'Ryan, don't lie just because you're feeling sorry for me,' she pleaded. 'Just admit that you were wrong, you don't want me now you know the truth and let's part friends, can we? I just want you to forgive me for deceiving you and not hate me for the rest of your life. I can live without you if I have to, but I can't live with your hate. It's destroying me, inch by inch…'

She closed her eyes and turned away, but not before the hot tears spilled down over her cheeks and ran into her hair.

She felt his hands on her shoulders, gathering her up against his chest, and then that chest moved in a huge, shuddering sob and his face was buried against her neck and he was crushing the life out of her.

'Don't,' he protested raggedly. 'Oh, hell, honey, don't cry. I don't hate you. I couldn't manage to hate you even when I thought you were just using my kids. How could I hate you for just simply trying to steal a little happiness?'

'I should have told you,' she mumbled into his shoulder.

'And I should have talked to you, instead of jumping to conclusions and saying all those terrible things to you.' He eased away and looked down at her, and his eyes were racked with guilt and pain and love.

'Virginia, can we start over?' he murmured. 'I love you. I don't care that you can't have children, except for you— because you're missing so much and it's so terribly, heart-breakingly sad that you had that taken away from you. I want to be with you, every minute of my life. Without you I'm nothing. My children love you; they miss you too. Come back to us—please? Come and play happy families again because we just aren't one without you. Please? I'm begging you, Virginia.'

She looked up into his eyes, hardly able to believe the love she saw there. 'I thought I'd lost you,' she whispered brokenly. 'I thought you were dead and I'd never see you again, and you would have died hating me, and I wanted to die too. I didn't care if it fell on me—not if you were in there. You don't have to plead with me, Ryan—in fact, you're going to have to shoot me to get rid of me because there's no way I'm going to let you go again.'

His arms slid round her and lifted her up against his chest. 'Relax,' he murmured. 'I'm not about to shoot you. Not now, not ever. You're mine, Virginia—mine and the children's. I was right—you are the perfect wife and mother, and if I have to spend the next however many years convincing you I'll do it willingly. Just be there for me—for us. That's all I ask.'

She swallowed the huge lump in her throat.

'That's easy. Consider it done, O'Connor.'

And, turning her head just a fraction, she kissed him…

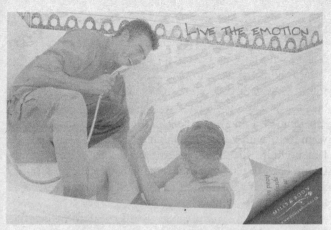

Modern Romance™
...international affairs
– seduction and
passion guaranteed

Medical Romance™
...pulse-raising
romance – heart-
racing medical drama

Tender Romance™
...sparkling, emotional,
feel-good romance

Sensual Romance™
...teasing, tempting,
provocatively playful

Historical Romance™
...rich, vivid and
passionate

Blaze Romance™
...scorching hot
sexy reads

30 new titles every month.

Live the emotion

MILLS & BOON®

Sensual Romance™

4 brand new titles each month

...teasing,
tempting,
provocatively
playful.

Available on subscription every month
from the Reader Service™

GEN/21/RS3

Historical Romance™
4 brand new titles each month
...rich, vivid
and passionate
Available on subscription every month
from the Reader Service™
GEN/04/RS3